Being a Rock Star wasn't always easy…

Penelope's little sister, Erica Princeton is beautiful, famous, and talented. As the singer in a wildly popular band, Erica's life seems perfect. But even super stars have problems. Tragedy, unrequited love, and rivalry make Erica realize there is more to life than fame and fortune in Los Angeles. Searching for meaning, purpose, and possibly a better life, Erica joins her family in her quaint hometown for a visit.

Penelope Princeton is big sister to Erica, the famous front singer in a popular punk/ska band, Flying Foes, based in Los Angeles After the death of Erica's good friend, lead guitarist Jim Jackson, Erica discovers she isn't as satisfied with her life as she thought. Her non-commital "boyfriend" of three years, Malcolm Jamison Smithe, a wealthy producer, can see nothing beyond the next album. Worse, her fans seem to think Erica is partly responsible for the death of Jim.

Searching for meaning, purpose, and possibly a better life Erica joins her sister and parents in her childhood hometown for a visit. Though it is in the middle of nowhere, she discovers that life can be richer and more satisfying away from the fame and drama of L.A. Along the way she runs into Charlie Jones, her first crush, an intriguing contractor who is working on her parents' home. Though she still holds out hope for the cold and uncaring Malcolm, she soon realizes wealth and power are not everything, especially when introduced to the possibility of real love.

Rock on Sister

Walla Walla's Amazing Erica Princeton

Sara Van Donge

Rock on Sister: Walla Walla's Amazing Erica Princeton

For more information about the Ghost Mystery series or any other books by Sara Van Donge, visit our web page: www.platformpublishers.com or send an email to receive updates about upcoming books: saravandonge@gmail.com.

Books by Sara Van Donge

Nonfiction:
Secrets to Educational Success: How YOU Can Be An A+ Student

Books for Adults
Dutch Jo and Her Good Time Girls
Rock On Sister: The Amazing Erica Princeton

Humorous Essays
I Love Love Walla Walla: Growing Up in the Town So Nice They Named It Twice

Books for Children

The Ghost Mystery Series:
The Green Lake Ghost
The Cemetery Ghost
The School Ghost
The Haunted House
The Park Ghost
Books are available at bookstores or at Amazon, follow this link:
http://www.amazon.com/Sara-Van-Donge/e/B00O0FXCCE

Dedicated to my own siblings. You are all rock stars.

Rock on Sister

Walla Walla's Amazing Erica Princeton

By Sara Van Donge

10th Anniversary Concert

2014

Maybe if I hadn't just gotten my hair done the day I met
Ricky none of this would have happened. But I guess that's just
me, blaming myself for something I had no control over.
Besides…I'm getting ahead of myself. Let me back up a little
bit and tell you about Erica. Because, well, everything always
comes back to Erica.

And why wouldn't it? Erica Princeton is beautiful. Erica
Princeton is talented. Erica Princeton is known all over the
world. On this spring Saturday night she was playing at Queen
Stadium in Los Angeles and the crowd was going wild. It was
her 10th year playing with The Flying Foes and they were more
famous now than ever. Her long blonde hair swinging jauntily as
she danced up and down the stage, Erica's throaty voice filled
the stadium. She beamed with pleasure as she saw young
teenagers dancing alongside middle-aged women, screaming all
the lyrics to her songs.

And Penelope Princeton? Well, that's me. I'm Penny, sister
to Erica Princeton, and decidedly NOT known all over the world.
Now, not for one second would I want you to think I have a
problem with this. I never wanted to be famous, I always left
that to my little sister. When she was 5 and I was 7 she stood on

a table at our grandparents' 50th wedding anniversary and belted out 'As Time Goes By' for their famous and powerful Hollywood guests. Me? I hid behind a curtain, watching and drawing pictures of the ladies' fancy dresses. I guess you could say Erica and I are a good match.

On this Friday night in Los Angeles I stood just off stage, directing our costume crew to help Erica with one of her many quick changes. Erica looked over her shoulder at her band. Jim Jackson, her best friend and the lead guitarist winked at her as he led the crowd in a cheer. Ben Beirne, the bassist, smiled as he kept rhythm for the group, singing harmony along with Erica and Jim.

Jim tore off his shirt during Carlisle's 30 second drum solo following the song, the roar of the crowd increased substantially as he strutted around the stage showing his wiry physique. Erica caught the eye of his wife, Kelly, who was standing just off stage. The old friends shared a smile at the antics of Jimmy. Both were used to seeing the wild and crazy side of the famous Jim Jackson and it was welcome - though too much could get out of control and scary. But they didn't have to worry, Jim's out of control days were behind them. Erica shimmied up next to her long-time band member and sang the lead while he harmonized, picking up each note and making it stronger. I could tell she was really feeling the energy of the crowd and it was making her energy level soar. She glanced briefly towards the wing of the stage, the slightest bit of worry crossing her face. I rolled my eyes. I knew she was hoping to see Malcolm Jamison Smithe, her on-again, off-again boyfriend. It seemed they were more off-again than anything else, but she somehow couldn't let him go completely. The more he disappointed her the more she wished she could count on him.

Earlier that afternoon, as they had worked with all of us on their team helping with sound checks and placement of instruments, Erica had been worried. She had sent Malcolm a text.

<How are you?>

He had never responded. Here she was, dancing in front of 20,000 fans on stage at Queen Stadium, singing her Grammy-winning hit to an enthusiastic crowd at a sold-out concert…and was she thinking about how cool it was? No. Instead she was fretting about Malcolm. He hadn't shown up (again!) and now she was wondering once again why he wouldn't commit to her. Even though Erica kept her insecurity to herself, I knew her well enough to see she was struggling.

She was embarrassed to be doing the text game with Malcolm. If Jimmy, Ben or Carlisle had any idea she was still texting and worrying about Malcolm they would never let her live it down. After three years they were so fed up with his hot and cold that they refused to even listen to her talk about him.

When they had finally played their last set, taken their last encore, and were relaxing in the lounge backstage, Jim kept repeating over and over, "Man, that was the best!"

Everyone else laughed. Carlisle still had his drum sticks and the bassist, Ben, played a slow blues-y baseline, not something they'd probably be able to slip past their hardcore punk and ska fans. Erica joined in with a mournful blues ballad, though with cheerful lyrics as Jim jammed on top with his guitar.

They were dissolving into laughter when a light tap at the door revealed an attractive couple who slipped through the door. Nearly androgynous in their beauty, I recognized the couple at once and sucked in my breath in shock. No. They can't be here.

Regular Kid...Sort Of

Guitar playing, free-thinking, handsome, charming Jim Jackson was not just the lead guitarist for Flying Foes, but also the glue holding the group together. More photographed than the rest put together, his antics both on and off stage created an air of mystery that people wanted to own. Jim was Flying Foes.

Jim Jackson and Erica Princeton had been best friends since they met almost fifteen years ago as thirteen year old stars on the wildly famous 'Kids Rock' TV program. Both had been raised by famous parents and had experienced the joys and difficulties that come with being the child of superstars. Unlike Erica and me, whose parents had attempted to give us a "normal" life by moving us to a small town far from the fame, Jim's parents were both well-known movie stars who had reveled in the Hollywood lifestyle. From his earliest memory Jim had been surrounded by photographers and excited fans, unable to go out in public unless it was a well-orchestrated publicity stunt. He envied kids who were able to go to school, go downtown, go anywhere without being constantly scrutinized. Like Erica and me, Jimmy had enjoyed a pleasant childhood with kind and loving parents, but both of his parents were busy filming most of the time. His parents were one of the rare Hollywood couples that actually got along and enjoyed spending time together. So they went out of their way to get jobs on movies together or to stagger their filming so they could be there with the kids. Together with his younger sister Michelle, Jim had spent his childhood traveling to different exotic locations for filming interspersed with long vacations at their Canary Island estate or in their Mulholland Drive Mansion. However, unlike Erica, Jim had never had the chance to just be a regular kid. He had never attended school, his parents hadn't trusted his safety. Not to mention they were just too busy filming and hadn't wanted their kids raised by nannies and tutors. His mother Hillary Jackson had starred for five years as an actress on a popular TV show before moving on to make movies, winning an Oscar when Jimmy was fourteen.

Though his mother was America's Sweetheart, one of the most recognized women in the world, Jim simply knew her as mom and as a child had wished he could spend more time with her. His father, Hank Jackson, also a famous actor, known for his action films and thrillers, was a sought-after star like his wife. So between the two of them Jim had spent a lot of his childhood on movie sets. By the time he was five directors had discovered Jimmy Jackson as an actor in his own right and began putting him in his parents' films. But it was when Jim started writing music, playing the guitar alone while waiting for his tutors or handlers to direct him to the next activity that he discovered his true passion and talent.

Soon, Jim was entertaining the crew while he waited for his parents to film scenes. And not too long after that he was making his own TV show, performing for his own audiences. He became famous for being himself, rather than the son of two movie stars. But Erica had given Jim the taste for a normal life when she described her three years of elementary school in a sweet little town called Walla Walla. Our parents owned an understated Tudor on a quaint street near the downtown. Once she became famous Erica would come visit us if her schedule gave her a couple of days.

When Jim discovered that Erica had lived in Walla Walla before moving to Los Angeles permanently to begin filming Kids Rock he had teased her playfully. What kind of podunk town is called Walla Walla? Why would the famous producer Bruce Princeton and movie star Adelaide Princeton move away from glamorous Hollywood to go there? But Erica was ready with her bright smile and positive energy. She gently guided Jim to understand how nice it had been to just be a regular kid. Though she hadn't really been a regular kid, she had been pretending…but still, she got to pretend and Jim never had.

So when he was fifteen and his parents told him they were planning to spend Christmas on location in Toledo he decided to join Erica, me, and our parents in Walla Walla. He was surprised at how much he loved it. Because it was a small town where famous people rarely set foot, then the people didn't expect you to be famous or barely noticed. Sure, Jim got some looks, as if people in a coffee shop or a bookstore recognized him. But then they would just shake their head as if they knew there was no way that could be Jim Jackson, child star. Why would he be in Walla Walla?

Of course, when Jim, Erica, and I walked downtown or played basketball at the local YMCA or went out for lunch they ran double the risk of being recognized. But they were both so happy to not be famous for a few days, to not be photographed in their sweats or eating junk food, that they purposefully underdressed so people would just assume they were students and not give them a second look. And Walla Walla became their hideaway.

When Jim's parents and sister Michelle could, they joined him. Though once his parents flew into the small airport in a private airplane the local newspaper caught wind of the excitement and readily identified them. So Jim and Erica's cover was blown and they were no longer incognito, not that they could have remained invisible for long, even in a small town where no one expects someone famous. But it didn't really matter, people in the Pacific Northwest, and especially in small farming communities, pride themselves first and foremost on treating each other with respect. So they were left alone.

During this time I enjoyed a regular life, attending the smallish pubic schools, taking art classes, and working behind the scenes for our school theater. Unlike my sister, I was perfectly content to quietly watch and help when it came to performances and I found a niche in the theater department helping with lights, stage management, and my favorite: costumes. Many kids seemed unaware of my younger sister's fame and I certainly wasn't going to remind anyone. I stuck to my small group of friends, nursed an unrequited crush that I was too shy to do anything about, and sailed through high school pretty unscathed.

A few times a year my parents would pack up in a flurry so we could all go to L.A. with Erica. We would visit the set, enjoy our California cousins, and usually go to some type of award show. Erica only had to be in Los Angeles for filming, so one of my parents would usually just go with her, leaving the rest of the time for enjoying the sights of the city. But all of us were always happy to return home to the quiet peace of our little hometown.

By the time they were seventeen Kids Rock completed it's final season, as popular the last day of the series as the first. Erica and Jim were ready to take their creative lives into their own hands. While they had been working together on the show they had often written and played music while waiting for scenes. Erica had a gift for lyrics and harmony that corresponded perfectly with Jimmy's guitar-playing genius. Together they created songs that the entire cast and crew looked forward to listening to. The show was based on music and had three or four choreographed musical numbers interspersed throughout each episode centering around a group of teens living and studying at an elite boarding school. Erica and Jimmy were the only two that had any enduring musical talent, though. The other cast members could sing a little, but were mainly hired for their good looks and dancing abilities. It made for a good mix, and created a show that fans loved tuning into each week.

I had always enjoyed watching the show, mainly to look for signs of the evil I knew was lurking beneath the surface of Roxana Shilling, the beautiful young actress who played Erica's best friend on the show. Erica had only been working three days when she had called me in tears to ask for advice on how to deal with the actress portraying her best friend.

"She is amazing, I'll give you that." Erica had sobbed, generous to a fault. "When the cameras are rolling she is all light and smiles and even I start to believe she likes me. Then the director yells cut and her eyes just glaze over, like she can't even see me."

I was in my first year of high school at this point and used to mean girls, though none at the level of the wealthy and amazing Roxana Shilling. Still, I figured a mean girl is a mean girl.

"Just be nice to her, let her make herself look bad." Was all I could offer.

Other than Roxana, once she began Kids Rock Erica was thrilled with her new life in Los Angeles. She was living with family in Lost Angeles and our parents and I saw her often, plus she had made friends (not a boyfriend!) with a guy named Jim. I was happy for her, though I missed her.

Ricky

While she was filming Kids Rock, Erica also talked to me about was a guy named Ricky Rhodes. He hadn't appeared on the show until 2002, in the third season. He quickly made an impression on my sister as someone I might like.

"He's really cool, Pen, he's perfect for you. He's this amazing athlete - and none of those bonehead sports all the guys up there think are so important either. He skates in empty swimming pools on our days off, he golfs, he goes rock climbing and has even been sky diving a few times. Plus you should see him dance."

By this point Erica had settled into the routine of being on a very popular show and she was thoroughly enjoying it. I was a senior in high school and my busy schedule kept me from spending as much time as I would like with my sister in Los Angeles. But we were always close and I enjoyed listening to her stories of fame and excitement in L.A. I shared my stories of band practice and homework too, but somehow they weren't quite the same.

For spring break that year I flew with my mom to visit Erica and I met Ricky. We instantly hit it off. His long dark hair and brooding eyes were just the right mixture of cool and gorgeous and I was instantly smitten. More than smitten, I was lovestruck. But the crazy thing was he liked me back.

Maybe I shouldn't be so down on myself, I mean it's not like I'm not cute or nice or fun to be around. My family and small group of close friends all really love me. I have nice blonde hair that's straight and healthy - though in those days straight healthy hair wasn't as cool as great big bouncy hair, or at least that's what I was always aiming for. And I have a nice figure, in fact Erica is often lauded for her amazing figure and she and I can share clothes. But she exercises for at least an hour every single day and I feel amazing if I take a ten minute walk, so guess whose butt is tighter? But in high school I was considered bookish. I wore these really incredibly unattractive glasses and I was just simply unsure of myself when it came to guys.

But Ricky liked me. Ricky liked me! He spotted me with my mom as soon as I walked in, I could tell. You know that look a guy gives when he's interested? That lingering look, but if he's cool he won't let you catch him staring? He was doing that. I was wearing a Beatles shirt and my favorite jeans plus my mom had just insisted on taking me to her favorite salon for a "blow out" which is basically just paying someone to wash and dry your hair. I guess I looked good.

By the time Erica got around to introducing us he was eager to talk to me, he kept coming up with excuses to break away from their dance practice or blocking to come over and ask me questions. By the time mom and I left the studio he had managed to get my phone number.

I was wary. I never really trusted good-looking guys and this one was on a really popular TV show to boot. But the more I pushed him away and found excuses not to return his calls, the harder he tried to get to know me. I saw him a couple more times over the summer and when I moved to Los Angeles that fall to study costume and set design at UCLA he was already calling himself my boyfriend.

Ricky was cool. He had lived in the Valley as a child, the son of a bartender. Ricky had spent his youth bouncing around with his mom, crashing elite parties. His youthful confidence and handsome good looks allowed him to float seamlessly between his wild world and the prestige of Hollywood.

We had fun. We would go thrift store shopping and watch movies. And make out. A lot. He was my first real boyfriend and our passion consumed both of us. I tried to ignore the fact that he didn't have a very good work ethic or that he would disappear for days at a time without an explanation. He appeared on Kids Rock for only one season as a dancer before being fired for excessive partying. By this point Erica regretted having mentioned him to me, she had seen him go from being really talented on the show to being unreliable and even rude at times.

But the more she tried to talk to me about him, the more I defended him. With me he was always someone I could count on, or at least someone I could count on to have a really good excuse if he didn't follow through when he should. Erica accepted him and they got along. Although I suspected she didn't entirely trust him.

To make matters worse for Erica, Ricky and Jim had remained good friends. Jim would sometimes disappear for a few days with Ricky, returning a little worse for the wear. Despite Erica's growing disapproval, Jim always insisted they weren't doing anything they shouldn't. By the time Kids Rock had finished up its final season in 2004, Ricky and I were married. Jim and Erica and other friends would sometimes join us for dinners or parties and Erica began to accept my new husband, although she always kept him at arms length.

The Flying Foes

Once they were no longer filming Kids Rock, Erica suggested she and Jim sing together. Her lyrics and songs together with his music on the guitar. They had thrown themselves into the idea of a band with the same amount of gusto they had previously dedicated to the song and dance numbers on the show. When they began looking for the rest of their band, they had easily found Ben Beirne, their bassist. Ben was a few years older than Erica and Jim and had been playing in lesser-known bands throughout L.A. for a half a dozen years before Erica's agent suggested they meet with him. It had been instantly comfortable with Ben and they had begun writing songs together.

But a guitarist, a bass player, and a singer - even though very talented - do not make a band. The group, now called the Flying Foes, needed a drummer. The next few months looking for a drummer were fun. Even if laws are still supposed to apply to famous people and, being 17, Erica and Jim shouldn't have, they managed to get into a lot of popular music venues. By bringing along their agents and managers and other important people and creating an entourage scene the burgeoning rock stars were able to peruse all the most popular clubs in search of their drummer. But nothing ever seemed to work out, either the guy would be very interested in them but wouldn't be interested in their brand of ska/punk or they would find someone suitable but he would already be committed to a group and unable to join the Flying Foes.

It was after two months of unsuccessfully searching, attending different evening concerts around Southern California, listening to recorded demonstrations from hopeful drummers, and scouring every other source of musicians they could think of that they decided to take a vacation. Erica thought we should all go to Walla Walla. So that summer, Jim, Ben, Ricky and I flew to Walla Walla. Ben, who had never even been out of California, much less a tiny town on the other side of the country, was surprised when we flew into the little airport.

"Wow," Ben said, as we stepped out of the turbo-prop airplane and walked across the tarmac to the tiny airport, "this is…something."

I looked around my hometown, trying to see it through his eyes, and I had to laugh. Yes, the Blue Mountains visible nearby just past the golden wheat fields were beautiful, but compared to the bustle and sophistication of Los Angeles, this was really uncultured.

In California, Erica and Jim felt the constant pressure to perform and succeed. To look and act like the stars everyone needed them to be. And it was fun. It was fun to wear the latest fashions, everything always brand-new and beautiful. It was fun to have thousands of people want to talk to you and take your picture. It was fun to pull up in front of the coolest club in Hollywood, get out of a limo, and have the crowd part so you can just walk right in. But it was hectic to always have to be on, to always be on the lookout for cameras and what people think.

In Walla Walla they could relax, despite the fame. Somehow the people of our small town had decided to just let the Princetons and the Jacksons just be. Everyone was friendly, they extended the same courtesy toward the famous people from L.A. that they bestowed on anyone. But no one ever bothered them for an autograph or a picture. Being in Walla Walla was home.

This July in 2004 we arrived in Walla Walla to take a break from the never ending search for the perfect band member. I think Ben and Jim were starting to worry about working with Erica. She could be pretty type-A and demanding, a little known fact hidden by her usual cheer. But her determination to find the perfect fit for their newly forming band was putting a lot of pressure on all of them, as well as taking time aways from any potential performances they might be playing.

I had confidence in her, though. If anyone could make a band achieve it was my little sister. From earliest childhood she had been organizing shows, though usually she was the producer, director, and star. I had always been her audience and this time I was prepared to watch her shine for the rest of the world too.

Young Love

I married Ricky earlier that same year, when I was 19. After 2 years of dating, we decided to get married. Why? Well, obviously, I got pregnant. I know there were other things we could have done - believe me, everybody had a suggestion. But I missed him whenever I went to visit my parents. And I thought having a big party to celebrate our love sounded like a fun thing to do. Plus he was willing. All really good reasons to get married, right? Oh, no? Ricky hadn't grown up with a dad and he had this mistaken notion of marriage being a salve for everything, so I guess that's why he was OK with it. Or maybe he liked the security of my family money. Me? I think I was just caught up in the fever of having a baby and a family. Though I have to admit I didn't really think it through. We never actually had an intelligent conversation about the whole scheme.

I was back in Los Angeles after a visit with my parents in Walla Walla. They hadn't been too excited about my surprise news, though admittedly I hadn't been at first, either. But there's something calming about being pregnant, my body just kind of took over and I wanted stability. Plus Ricky and I had missed each other terribly, talking on the phone frequently each day, and we were thrilled to be reunited. We were driving in my L.A. Jeep, going to visit my cousins when the subject of marriage came up. With almost no fanfare we ended up deciding to go for it. It was a conversation something like this:

Me: "Where do you think you will live after this baby comes?"

Ricky: "I don't know, somewhere near you. I don't like being away from you. Maybe we could live together."

Me: "I guess we could get married."

Ricky: "Yeah, that's a good idea. Should we just do that?"

Me: "OK. We should probably do it in Walla Walla, my mom would like that."

So we decided to get married. Six weeks later. And once Ricky's family found out it was a done deal and there was no turning back. I had some serious second thoughts, too. But immediately his mom and aunt and cousins started eagerly volunteering to make the invitations, sing in the ceremony, take pictures, bake the cake, make appetizers, you name it…well there was no turning back. From the moment the words left my lips….my life was on a trajectory I could not control.

The marriage may have been less than ideal, but the wedding was great! My family really came through and gave a big shindig. After the traditional ceremony in front of a packed crowd in my childhood church everybody drove out to the Walla Walla Country Club which was one of the biggest places in town, something we needed to accommodate our huge family. Ricky's family was all from California, but since there weren't too many of them my dad just flew them out for the week.

Erica wasn't too happy with the idea of our marriage, but she put on a good face for me. She and Jim had been practicing a lot on their own and they played at the reception. We ate a tremendous amount of food made by all the best local chefs. We topped our cake with Homer and Marge Simpson and had a candy table. Later we moved the party down the street to an elegant downtown bar where my parents had set up karaoke. This was one of the first times I had ever done karaoke and I was hooked from the start. We sang 'We are Family,' 'Space Cowboy,' and 'Girls Just Wanna Have Fun'. I had never liked performing in front of people, but singing with my family was pretty fun.

We had so much fun that night, ending up with an elaborately decorated limo taking us to the airport so we could head off for two weeks in Hawaii.

Everything should have been great from here, right? But it wasn't. We had been married for fifteen days when Ricky received a letter from Roxana Shilling. Of all people! We had been home from our Hawaiian honeymoon for exactly one day and had just begun to settle in to our new apartment in Los Angeles. I had made the (unwise, immature) decision to take the term off from school and was planning to spend my days enjoying my newly wedded bliss.

But when the pink envelope arrived in our mailbox I was confused. I carried it upstairs, reading and re-reading the return address. Roxana Shilling. Roxana? That horrible girl from Kids Rock? Erica's nemesis? Writing to my new husband? Why would she be writing to my husband? And it was written in a stupid swirly cursive I instantly hated.

I brought it upstairs and set it on the table, wanting to just ignore it. Ricky was out, something he had always done in our two years of dating, something I chose not to think about. But I couldn't ignore this letter, it called to me from the table as I arranged our new dishes into our new kitchen. It called to me as I folded our new towels into our new hall closet. It called to me as two hours later Ricky still hadn't returned from his unspecified outing.

I tore it open.

Roxana wrote to Ricky in her loopy, easy-to-read big cursive, saying she'd heard about his wedding. She asked why he'd gotten married when he loved her and they were still together? I sank to the floor as I realized she still considered herself his girlfriend. They had started dating before he even met me, back when they were filming Kids Rock together. And he hadn't really ever gotten around to breaking up with her before he and I had started dating two years before. I got it, having two girlfriends is always so much more convenient than just one.

I sat there on the floor, reading and re-reading the letter. Apparently Roxana (who used the word alas, alas! three separate times in the letter) had been pregnant the previous spring and Ricky had taken her to get an abortion. She talked of still loving him, needing him to come back to her. Then the line that made me feel the sickest:

How can you be with that square who doesn't even know you use smack?

Smack? Like heroine? Was that what he would disappear to do? Was that why he went through money so quickly? Smack? How could this be happening?

I knew I should leave, I should call my parents and admit my mistake. Call Erica, tell her she was right and Ricky was as bad - no worse - than she had told me. She had often been so distraught about Roxana, she would absolutely sympathize.

But, logic prevailed and I had a mountain of wedding gifts to sort through and write thank-you cards for. And the thought of admitting to our 250 guests that, oops, my new husband was a cad was just too overwhelming to me. Not to mention I was three months pregnant. So I hunkered down and tried to pretend nothing was wrong. By the time he came home I had hidden the letter, he never knew she had written to him. But I watched him, and I tried to figure out what to do.

Drummer

So that July, as Ricky and I were visiting Walla Walla with Erica, Jim, and Ben, I had to pretend I was happy. I don't know why, I should have just told my little sister what had happened and things probably would have turned out so much differently for me. But she was so excited about her newly forming band, she was so full of life and fun, that I just didn't think about it. I loved my great big belly and felt happy and could almost pretend that I had never read that horrible letter from Ricky's (ex?) girlfriend.

And even though I was upset at Ricky and I wasn't sure if our marriage had been a good idea, we had always loved having fun together. So as we walked with Erica, Jim, and Ben from our parents mansion the few blocks to downtown we were all full of enthusiasm and good cheer. Even me, in the summer heat at 7 months pregnant.

We heard music coming from Main Street before we got to the street dance. We could hear blues-y rockabilly music filling the balmy air. The white lights glimmering on the trees were shining in Erica's eyes.

"Do you hear that Jimmy? Do you?" Erica danced around her friends, gleeful at hearing what sounded like a really great band playing music. Their style of music.

Jim and Ben both laughed. Erica was not just a dedicated performer, intent upon seeing their fledgling band take off, she was also just a lot of fun.

When we walked into the roped off area in front of the street, no one noticed Erica or Jim were famous. Erica had so much fun, dancing all over the room. She was enjoying not only the excellent sounding drum beat, but the entire band. This is just what they had been waiting for.

Then suddenly Erica was still, her eyes were wide as she noticed a dark-haired, broad shouldered man sitting nearby. He was staring at her, in fact he had been staring at her for awhile and she hadn't registered it. Her joyful expression had melted into one of panic and nerves, two emotions Erica rarely showed.

"What is it? Is there a problem?" Jim, always the good friend, had noticed the change in Erica.

"It's Charlie Jones." She whispered, barely audible above the still bopping music. Her eyes were on the guy. Even though she answered Jim she hadn't looked away.

Without any further clarification, she stepped toward the handsome man, dragging me with her. When she reached his table, still intently looking at him, she appeared to shake off the anxiety she had been feeling. Like the talented actress she is Erica greeted the young man with an exuberant hug, calling out his name so happily that people at nearby tables all looked over to see what the excitement was about.

"I haven't seen you since the sixth grade, Charlie Jones!" Erica's charm was turned on full blast now and anyone watching wouldn't be able to miss the effect it was having on the young man. He squirmed happily under her flirtatious gaze, smiling down at her then nodding politely to me too.

"I heard you came to visit Walla Walla sometimes," he said shyly looking at the table before continuing on, "I hoped I might run into you at some point."

The music was loud enough that they had to put their faces close together and talk right into one another's ear. Erica put her hand on Charlie's muscular upper arm as she leaned in.

"I hoped you were still here too, do you still live here?"

As Charlie was explaining about his training to be a carpenter, working as an apprentice, his eyes shone. He described his work, working on building quality houses and I saw Erica settling comfortably next to him, she seemed intrigued by the normalcy of his work and his passion for it. Just then, a young woman appeared, carrying a drink and wearing a big scowl. She was older than both Erica or Charlie and she was clearly not happy to see a rival. Positioning herself aggressively between Erica and Charlie, the older woman put a proprietary hand on Charlie's shoulder and leaned in to whisper to him.

Erica spun back toward the dance floor, waving toward Charlie as we left to join Ben and Jim. Both had witnessed the scene and dissolved into teasing laughter as soon as we returned to their table next to the stage. Erica danced, both alone and with anyone else who was dancing, for the rest of the show. She could probably feel Charlie's eyes on her. She even looked over at him a few times and flashed a smile, which he returned in a friendly way. But I knew my sister, she wasn't interested in a man with a girlfriend, so she appeared to push him out of her mind.

After the band had finished playing Jim, Erica, and Ben asked the drummer if he had a card so they might contact him. He turned his head quizzically to the side.

"A card?" He asked, his pale skin standing out against the darkness of the crowded club.

It turned out the drummer, named Carlisle Chicken (Chicken? Seriously?) had only recently begun playing in front of people, at the urging of his sister, Jenna. At this, Carlisle, who was quiet and seemed overwhelmed by three people clamoring for information from him, gestured to a young woman sitting at a table nearby. She had his same striking pale skin and blue eyes. She was sitting with two other young women, deep in conversation. She threw her head back and laughed at something her friend was saying when she looked over and saw Carlisle beckoning her. She excused herself and came bustling over.

Carlisle seemed at a loss, he gestured toward Ben with a shrug, clearly hoping his sister would take charge of the situation. Jenna looked at Ben and then at Erica and her face registered recognition.

She laughed, "Carlisle, are you star struck?" She gave her brother, who must have been at least three years younger, a playful punch on the arm.

Jenna turned to Ben, shook his hand, and then with the same confident smile she turned toward Erica and then Jim. She was aware of their fame, but she seemed determined to make nothing of it.

Erica arranged for their manager to call Carlisle, leaving the still silent drummer staring at them as his sister teasingly pushed him back up on the stage to finish his set. Once he got back into the groove, though, he seemed to forget all about the conversation and quickly fell back into his drummer trance. I had to admit, he would be a great addition to the band. Erica was looking wistfully over at the at the table, now empty, where Charlie had been sitting. Ricky and Jim returned with coffee from a nearby coffee shop.

After thanking them, she sighed. Then shook her head, seeming to force whatever sad thoughts were bothering her out of her head.

"You remember Charlie, right?" She asked.

"Of course, you were so silly about him in school."

Erica shook her head. "Darn it, why do all the good ones always end up with girlfriends."

I laughed. "You don't have time to be anyone's girlfriend! But if you wanted to be with someone, you could."

She smiled at me, moving her shoulders to the fun music Carlisle's band was belting out. "You're right, what am I thinking. To the Flying Foes!"

She picked up her coffee and toasted cups with me and then with Ben, who was deep in conversation with Jenna. Then she shimmied out onto the dance floor, starting out alone but soon joined by a whole crowd of people. Erica's positive energy was always infectious.

Sorry Penny

The next couple of months were very lonely, I was missing Walla Walla and wishing I could just move home. I wanted to be near my mom when I had my baby, especially since Ricky didn't seem very interested. I was unhappily married and couldn't admit it to anyone.

Erica by this point had started to really take off with The Flying Foes, and she was trying to get me to work with her to help her develop her style. I was going back to school, but I could hardly muster up the energy to do anything besides take a few classes. I must have been depressed.

Ricky wasn't terrible, not really. When I describe what happened later I feel this compulsion to describe the good times too - just so people can understand that he wasn't always terrible. Or maybe so my kids won't someday hear me and feel awful. Or maybe just to make myself feel better because I was such a wimp for staying married to someone who ignored me, threatened to hurt me, yelled at me, and spent a lot of his free time high. I mean, there are worse things, right? This is what I would tell myself whenever I actually thought of it, which I didn't.

But he did have his good qualities. On Saturdays when we were first married we would drive the 20 miles to the Fashion District and spend the day window shopping and going out to lunch, maybe going to a movie. We always enjoyed the same movies and would joke about them later. We had our references we could make with just a few words that would send us into peals of laughter.

But in those early months of marriage it wasn't usually very bad. We didn't have that much stress once I went back to school and we got into a regular routine. Besides caring for my ever-expanding belly, I had three design classes and I was helping Erica create her elaborate costumes. But being busy kept me numb from thinking about my personal life, so I guess this was good. Ricky was fairly busy too, he managed to find the occasional acting or dancing job. He and Jim were still friends, but Erica wasn't happy when they spent time together. She worried that Ricky was a bad influence.

For awhile we appeared to have it together. In fact, we really did have it together. Ricky and I had a few mutual friends, though he found my friends from school and other friends with families to be boring. I found a lot of his friends to be too rough. But once we had our son, Pearson, I longed for a more peaceful home life. I missed my family and wished we could move home, but Ricky refused. I went to visit them a lot, but it just wasn't the same.

Ricky struggled to find work, although since he had never really had a steady job this was nothing new. I tried to keep our struggles from my parents. My mom, the amazing Adelaide Princeton, had been so famous when I was young that we hadn't been able to go out in public without a huge commotion. She had made a fortune playing the cute leading blonde in a whole bunch of sweet romantic comedies in the late 1970's and all through the 80's. Though she had not wanted to retire (I remember her wailing when a younger rival actress was given a role she dearly wanted), my dad had encouraged her to bow out of the spotlight gracefully.

"Addie, you have seen too many actresses cling to fame for far too long. You can retire now, with dignity. Learn to enjoy other aspects of life." He had told her kindly.

This was when we had moved to Walla Walla and Dad was right, Mom did eventually learn to love life out of the spotlight.

But she still retained some of her movie star qualities, not the least of which was a certain self-centered narcissism. If I were to have revealed to my mother that my husband had a drug addiction, that he would regularly lose his temper and scream at me, and that he called me terrible names, she would have turned it into a big scandal. I doubt she would have helped me at all. So I pretended everything was great.

And in many ways everything really was pretty great. My father, being one of the most sought after producers in Hollywood, even after moving to the middle of nowhere, had set up trust funds for both Erica and me. So we never had to work and money was never an issue. We've been lucky. Not having to work, it has always given both of us the freedom to work at pursuits that we are passionate about.

After a few months Ricky found a niche working at a local dance studio, teaching jazz and hip hop classes and our life took on a comfortable rhythm. We got along well for the most part and I was pretty confident that he wouldn't lose his temper most of the time. Though every few months he would get angry and yell and twice he threatened to hurt me. Once he held a knife over his head while I lay on the ground crying, though he only threw it at me in the end. That night he wouldn't let me sleep and wouldn't let me call the police or leave the house. The next day when I went upstairs to my office to work, exhausted, I called a domestic violence hotline and the counsellor (who I know meant well, but ugh…) told me I was not in an abusive relationship because I controlled the money. Yes, because I was the person who most of the income, wrote all the checks, bought all the groceries, and made sure we didn't overdraw our checking account - I was in total control in the household. Being threatened with a knife didn't really matter since I could spend my trust fund and my earnings how I wanted. Thanks a lot, lady. I guess I must not have wanted to believe I wasn't safe or I would have just left. Instead, I stayed home and neither Ricky nor I ever said anything about it again; but we both knew he slept with the knife under his side of the mattress, and it wasn't to keep intruders out.

I dreamed of a better life but was under the mistaken impression that I would never find anyone else to love me. I could scream when I think of the folly in this logic. I was 20 years old and stayed in a miserable and frightening marriage because I was worried no one else would want me! I wish I could go back in time and shake my young self and make her see how stupid this logic is. Who cares? So what if no one had ever loved me again? I needed to love me. But, I guess that's the point, isn't it? I didn't love me.

After about a year of marriage Ricky stopped spending time with Pearson and me at all. One day he informed me that he needed time alone. He spent a lot of time in our basement. He sat at his computer for hours. He played golf almost daily at my Dad's Country Club. This was when he started spending all of his free time and ridiculous amounts of our money at the driving range and traveling to tournaments. I supported his hobby, I supported everything, but I missed his company. I should have searched for a friend at this point, huh? I wonder what was wrong with me? Instead I dreaded evenings because I spent them alone after Pearson had gone to sleep. I was pretty pathetic, I will never know what caused my lack of initiative. But I seemed to be frozen and miserable and unable to do anything to improve my situation.

But then I found something, or rather someone, to occupy my mind: my first love.

Erica Soars

That same summer of 2004, after meeting Carlisle, The Flying Foes decided to go to Portland, Oregon. Most musical groups just starting out try to get venues to host them, make frequent social media posts, and play often hoping people like them and talk about them. All with the goal of getting record companies to sign them. Erica and Jim didn't have this issue, in fact they had an almost opposite issue: they needed to establish that they were, in fact, legitimate musicians and not being catapulted to fame by their daddies' wealth.

So, yes, they could have gone right to Los Angeles, gotten signed on with one of the record labels owned by friends of either of their dads, and had their songs pushed to the front of the top 40 radio stations. Then spent the remainder of their careers enduring the wrath of people who accused them of becoming famous not through talent but through nepotism. So instead they went where the music scene was young and real and where people were so far removed from popular culture they could even try to be incognito. It wasn't Walla Walla, where they could have played completely unnoticed for visitors wine tasting, but Portland where the laid-back vibe and thriving music scene would give them a chance to be discovered for their true talent.

Not to mention, Carlisle was oblivious to the idea of being famous and was mainly interested in completing his degree in music theory at Portland State University. Erica and Jim had waited so long to find an available drummer who matched their style that they were willing to go to Portland. And once they arrived they realized it was a great city with a very appreciate music scene.

Erica invited us to watch one of their first big gigs. Pearson was tiny at this point and Ricky and I had left him at the hotel with my mom's sister Etta. It was the first time I had been away from my baby and I was trying not to be obsessed about checking my phone. I wanted to enjoy The Crystal Ballroom, a funky place downtown with a floating dance floor.

My mom was, of course, completely out of her element. Her platinum blonde hair was piled on her head, little tendrils curled prettily around her face. She wore a peach cashmere cardigan over a black silk jump suit and whenever one of the enthusiastic audience members bumped into her she would steady her white wine, put her hand over her heart and look at me, her lips pursed in discomfort. I probably screamed "It's OK mom!" over the din fifteen times.

Jenna, Carlisle's sister, was sitting with us. She caught my eye and smiled at my mom's antics. I had only been with Jen a few times and I really enjoyed her company. Where Carlisle was laid back and unconcerned with almost anything that wasn't music theory or drum solos, Jen was practical and down to earth. She could talk to anyone about anything and was a lot of fun.

My dad turned his hearing aid off and sat nodding happily, tapping his foot as if extremely loud music was his absolute favorite form of entertainment. I got a kick out of watching everyone enjoy my little sister and her band. The Flying Foes were good, very good, right from the beginning. They had an understanding of combining musical elements in a way that made every song not just catchy and fun, but harmonically and lyrically beautiful. I could see people standing up to dance who didn't look like they usually got out there on the dance floor, I saw people grinning and nodding to each other, I even saw two guys with multiple tattoos and piercings give each other a high five.

"This band kicks ass!" One yelled as the other screamed incoherently at the stage where Erica was strutting across the front like she owned it.

And she did, she was in her element and her joy in performing was palpable. She looked gorgeous, her blonde hair was blown out into a smooth sheet around her pretty face and the outfit we had put together was perfect: a pair of jeans that had a tiny a 12-inch inseam, meaning they just barely covered the top of her underwear showing off her prominent hip-bones. Her shirt (a term I use loosely) was really more a piece of silk with four ribbons strategically placed to allow it to be tied halter-style around her neck and ribs. Plus she had on spiky black heels and lots of silver jewelry. She was hot. And her voice was smooth and throaty and she harmonized perfectly with Jim and Ben while Carlisle kept it all tied together. The Flying Foes were on fire.

When they were ready for a break the crowd hollered, begging for more. Erica smiled and blew them a kiss.

"Do you guys have any idea how sweaty you all are?" She asked the crowd playfully. "You all clearly need a drink, and don't forget to tip your bartenders!"

Joining my parents and me at our table near the back of the crowded room she allowed her cocky confidence to drop for a moment.

"How was it? Did we sound OK? Nothing was out of sync? Too loud? Out of tune?" She asked me, reaching for my water glass and draining it in one huge gulp.

"You were excellent. Perfect." I told her seriously.

After drinking a second glass of water, she asked us how she looked.

"Your makeup is wilting a little, you're shiny and you have some mascara under your eye, but other than that you look fantastic." Our mom told her, whipping out her bag and smacking a puff of powder on Erica's forehead.

After accompanying her to the bathroom to refresh her makeup I returned to the table as she ran back on stage. The audience cheered even louder than before, they were clearly glad to see Erica and the guys again.

My dad patted my mom's hand and gave her a little smile, he knew how trying the loud noise was for her. Any slight physical discomfort was difficult for her. But she gave him a big grin, she was clearly proud of Erica and The Flying Foes. We all were.

Unrequited Love

Then there was my lackluster life. Sure, I went to Portland and Walla Walla sometimes, but I spent most of my days caring for little Pearson. Though I had been foolish to marry so young, I had managed to finish up my degree by working really hard and taking a lot of online classes. But at this point I wondered it I would ever do anything with costumes or set design, though with the way Erica talked about her plans for The Flying Foes I was feeling hopeful.

Ricky spent a lot of time in our dark, dreary basement, but I just turned my attention to our baby…and I distracted myself with thoughts of my first love.

And my first love? His name was Raymond Nelson and he was my classmate all through school. I had always thought he was cute with his dark brown hair and brown eyes. He was athletic and serious, but he also played the saxophone and sang in the choir. I think I knew a lot more about him than he did about me.

I first noticed him when we were in the 8th grade, he sat in front of me in English class. Unlike the other guys who would slide in late, making rude comments to each other or trying to get the class to laugh with dumb jokes, Raymond would always read a book before class started. As a big reader myself, I found this intriguing. I noticed he loved science fiction, a genre I didn't usually read. I was more into Nancy Drew mysteries at that point.

I liked how he paid attention, how he really seemed interested in learning, and how he was always polite. But it was when he stood up for Jason Sparks that I totally fell in love.

Jason Sparks was this guy mean kids would make fun of. He was an easy target with a whiny voice, overly-eager and nervous, and always staying after class to tell the teacher stories about his computer. The girls ignored him, but the guys liked to touch their fingers together and pretend it created a Spark, making a zzzzap! noise whenever he talked or walked by. Typical bully behavior, not really something you could call out but obviously meant for Jason.

But one afternoon, Jason was giving a report. Mr. Cannady loved making us give speeches, he thought it prepared us for the real world. Jason was talking about the benefits of one type of computer over another, and I admit, he wasn't very interesting. But the guys in the class kept holding up their fingers and making this tiny zzz noise, so imperceptible Mr. Cannady didn't even notice.

After like the tenth zzz we could all tell Jason was getting upset, even Mr. Cannady. But typical teacher, he had no idea what was happening, nor could he know that Jason had to deal with this all day long. In every class, at lunch, in the hall. Jason's face was getting red and he was starting to talk faster, trying to get it over with. I could see Mr. Cannady looking out at the class, trying to pinpoint who was making the stupid noise, but he still wasn't doing anything. But Raymond did.

Like a hero, Raymond spoke up. "Knock it off you guys. Making that noise is so stupid. Does it make you all feel better about yourselves to harass somebody else?" He was looking around the room at all the guys, his face firm and confident.

I could tell by the expressions on the guys' faces that they were embarrassed, Raymond had put them in their place.

After that, nobody made the dumb spark noise anymore. In fact nobody bugged Jason Sparks anymore. Raymond acted like he hadn't done anything, at the end of class he just picked up his backpack and his book and strode out.

That was the night I decided to write him a love letter. I wish I could say I had been a confident, cool eighth grader. One of those girls who enjoys middle school, who confidently flirts with guys, who has boyfriends and goes to cool parties. But I wasn't. I was quiet, with a handful of nice friends, and I got good grades. And when it came to guys I couldn't think of any better way to express my burning love than by writing this cute guy a note.

I spent so much time writing and re-writing, trying to think of the perfect words to express all I felt, but then I ended up writing a short note saying what a hero he was for standing up for Jason. I couldn't help adding that I liked watching him play football. Then I stuck the note in his binder when he got up to sharpen his pencil.

I never saw if he got it. I watched him throughout our entire English class, but he never opened the binder. I waited for him to respond or something, but he never did. I was crushed. As an adult I could look back and see how silly I was, thinking one little note would open up a relationship with an 8th grade boy who rarely spoke to anyone. For all I know he never even got the note.

I made one more effort, two years later, at Valentine's Day. By this point we were in high school. Raymond was still shy, still really good at football, and still spent any down-time in class with a book under his nose. Oh, and he was so cute. I never liked any other guy.

Our school had a Sadie Hawkins type Valentine's Day dance, where the girl asks the guy. My friends all knew about my years-long crush on Raymond and were encouraging me to ask him. We strategized for days about how I could do it. At school? In our math class? At lunch? I was thinking maybe a note, but Christina, Sharon, and Geri knew about my last attempt with a note and all vehemently negated that plan. So we decided I would call him.

I had never called a guy before. I was terrified. But we all met at my house and had a script written and each of us had a guy we planned to call to ask to the dance. Christina went first and within five minutes our friend Justin had agreed to go with her. Triumphant! We all gained confidence from this. Sharon went next and our script once again proved successful when her crush Terry readily said yes. Geri's was easy, she just had to call her boyfriend Jason, who of course said yes. This just left me. The three yeses gave me a little confidence as I dialed Raymond's number.

"This is Raymond." I was talking to him!

My heart started to pound, but I looked down at the script in my hand.

"Hi Raymond. This is Penny, from math."

"Oh hey." He didn't sound too excited. I considered just hanging up, but instead I took a deep breath.

"So, do you want to go to the Valentine's Dance?" I asked, hoping my voice wasn't too squeaky.

"With who?" He asked.

I looked at our script. We had written out a few different scenarios, just in case, but this was one we hadn't considered.

"Um..." I faltered. "With, me?"

"Oh!" He laughed. Oh, phew, I was so relieved. "Well maybe. When is it?"

Why was he making this so hard for me? I gave him the date for the dance.

"Oh, too bad, my parents are taking me out of town for my cousins wedding that weekend." He said. He sounded genuine, but my feelings were so crushed I could hardly finish the conversation.

"Well, ok, have fun then." I managed to get out. "Bye."

And I hung up.

I felt like an idiot! I was so mortified, I didn't want to talk to my friends about it. Of course when they got the story out of me they were so supportive and kind and assured me it didn't mean anything. But I managed to avoid speaking to Raymond about anything but school for the rest of high school. Oh, I still watched him, noticed what books he was reading, tried to sit near him. I went to football games just to see him play. And once in PE he even told Christina he liked working on group projects with me. But I still never let him know I liked him, it was just more comfortable that way.

But once I got married and had a baby I found myself thinking of him as I hid my miserable marriage from everyone in my life. I think I just had too much free time. Having a baby so young made it hard to find other moms to be friends with and my friends from before were really sweet. But they didn't want to hang out with me at home while my baby slept. And, well, Ricky was Ricky. So I had a lot of quiet evenings at home. To think. And somehow my thoughts would turn to Raymond.

I had kind of forgotten about Raymond in the excitement of meeting and dating and marrying Ricky, but now that the reality of my life had sunk in he was like an escape. Of course I never saw him, how would I? Not that it would matter if I did - I had never actually had a relationship or even a genuine conversation with him, but he was a distraction.

When I went home see my parents I would sometimes go out on the town with some of my more lively cousins, Chester and his wife Loreen, while my parents watched Pearson. And I may not have been Erica, but I eventually gained confidence and learned to enjoy dressing up and dancing. It was on my 21st birthday when I finally saw Raymond again.

He had gone off to college and had returned home as a P.E. Teacher. He was as cute as I remember and I eventually got up the nerve to talk to him. We had a pleasant conversation, catching up. I doubt he thought anything of it. But I thought about him afterward, and anytime after that I would look for him whenever I went to Walla Walla.

The theater distracted me, too. Los Angeles has many community theaters and I soon found a niche working in the costume rooms. I could usually bring Pearson during the day while I sewed and at night I didn't have to be there until after he was all tucked into bed. Ricky supported my interest in theater, he would watch the show usually more than once, giving me a lot of compliments on the costumes. I'm not sure why he was so supportive of me having fun, he supported me going home to visit my parents too. It's moments like this when I start to wonder if maybe I just deserved to be beaten and threatened because I was so obnoxiously depressed. But I only think that for a moment, then I see the folly. But I also see that Ricky wasn't all bad, he wasn't. He loved me and kissed me and told me great job. He watched me draw and sew and listened as I described my costumes for shows and for individual clients. He helped me throw cast parties, serving food and keeping music going and chatting about guests afterwards. He wasn't all bad, he just had this stupid temper and hated himself as much as I hated myself and it hurt both of us. It hurt everything.

And there were times I thought I should leave. But had I not stayed I would have never had my two children, so I am glad that I did. Every lonely or scared or bleak moment was worth it.

The Flying Foes Test their Wings

By 2005 Erica was settled into a fun life in Portland, dealing with her own unrequited love. I wonder what's with us Princeton girls? I always thought girls that pined away over unavailable men were supposed to be those that had daddy issues, right? But our dad has always been wonderful and he loves our mom. Even when we were younger, before he retired and settled into a quiet life in Walla Walla, he always tried to be home or had us travel with him. But maybe my sister and I just had bad luck. Who knows.

Either way, Erica and I talked on the phone a lot, usually about shows and costumes and family happenings. But for awhile there she was pretty into Charlie. She would tell me about her band and their latest shows and songs she was writing - for about five minutes. Then for about thirty minutes she would talk on and on about Charlie Jones.

Charlie. I remember her having such a crush on Charlie when we first moved to Walla Walla from Los Angeles. Erica was in the fourth grade, and he was in her class at school. She came home the first day, sat down at dinner, and told all of us that she was in love. My parents and I got such a good laugh out of that! She was hurt, though, because I think she meant it. To my dad's relief, she rarely spoke to Charlie. I think they might have pushed each other around on the playground a little, but her stories of him usually consisted of something funny or helpful he did in class.

She had been good friends with his little sister, Amanda, who was one year behind her in school. She and Amanda and our neighbor, Geri, were inseparable the three years Erica went to school in Walla Walla. She still got together with them whenever she visited Walla Walla, though she hadn't seen Charlie in years as far as I knew.

But when she got to Portland, Charlie came to a few of her concerts. Amanda was going to school at Portland State University and she had invited her big brother to visit her in Portland when he had a few days free from his busy construction work. Amanda invited her brother to see The Flying Foes play a concert and Erica was thrilled.

"I couldn't believe he was there Pen! Charlie! And he is cuter now than ever, he got big. Jim says he's fat, but I don't think so, he's like this big teddy bear with kind brown eyes and he was there!" Erica was gushing on the phone about him.

I had to laugh, she sounded as smitten as she had in elementary school.

"So? Did you talk to him? Does he know you love him?" I laughed.

"Shut up! I am Erica Princeton, rock star!" She said confidently, I could just imagine her tossing her long blonde hair as she twirled around her spacious living room.

"Rock star, huh?" I mused. "That was fast, you guys have only been playing a few months. And wasn't your last concert at a dentist's office?"

"It wasn't a dentist office!" She was probably sitting down now, I smiled hearing the indignation in her voice. I consider it my duty as a big sister to knock the perfect princess on her ass sometimes. "It was a banquet for dentists!"

I let her hear me laugh, "Go on, I know. Tell me about your big sexy bear. Did you at least flirt with him? Touch his chest? Lick your lips or whatever?"

"Not really, I tried to play it cool. Plus I'm not sure if he's still with that girl he was sitting with last summer and I didn't want to be all desperate and ask, so…."

"Well, don't be too cool." I advised, thinking of Raymond and my years of wishing I had the nerve to talk to him. And now my marriage to the wrong guy.

While The Flying Foes were developing their sound, playing their first concerts in Portland, Erica invited Amanda to live with her. Our parents went to visit Erica when she first arrived in Portland and had decided they absolutely had to have an apartment in the Pearl District, a newly renovated area downtown with unique shops and rooftop gardens. They purchased an amazing top floor penthouse apartment. Erica and Amanda enjoyed the soaring ceilings, everything creamy white, and enormous windows along the entire outer wall overlooking downtown. When my mom and I brought Pearson to visit that summer we enjoyed meals on the shady terrace looking out over the Willamette River.

Amanda was a perfect roommate for Erica. She was a hard worker who brought Erica down to Earth but also someone Erica could talk to and bounce ideas off of. Amanda was really shy and tended to get nervous about things that were scary or different, so she gave Erica a perspective that allowed her to appeal to a broad range of interests with her music. Jim and Ben were both hard-core, worldly LA types, full of creative ideas. And Carlisle had an understanding of music that ensured their music came together in a way that people appreciated without even knowing why they liked it. But it was Erica, with her lyrics and harmonies and beautiful voice and stage presence that tied the band together.

They started gathering a small following. It started with friends and family (or was it the dentists?) but within a few short months they were playing four and five nights a week at biggest clubs in town with lines of people waiting to get in. The Flying Foes were good and people knew it.

Black Leather Pants

I loved visiting Erica in Portland, seeing her excitement and helping her plan what she was going to wear. The guys were pretty receptive to our clothing suggestions, too, though Carlisle only wore dark blue jeans, a white tee-shirt and this harsh-looking black leather jacket that he took off just before each show, draping over a stand near his drums. Ben liked to wear dignified button-down shirts and slacks, to everyones horror, but he was a really down to earth guy and we couldn't do much to persuade him to change. He had started dating Jenna, Carlisle's sister, and she liked how he looked, so who were we to argue? Besides, I figured it was good to have the sweet foil tossed into the mix of heavy black leather and denim.

Jim managed to find a pair of black leather pants in a thrift store on Hawthorne and he figured out pretty quickly that once he was on stage playing a heavy riff the girls (and a good number of guys too) would go crazy when he took his shirt off. Jim wore his black hair in a variety of cool styles, mixing it up often enough that he could have gone into a second career as a hair stylist. We soon figured out why: Kelly Brown, a hot little hair dresser who worked at a salon downtown. She had long brown hair that looked like it hadn't been cut in years, ironic since she was surrounded by hair getting chopped off all day. Or maybe that's why. But everyone really enjoyed Kelly and she kept Jim's crazy antics at a minimum.

Because even though things were going great for him, Erica told me she was worried. She suspected he was using heroine.

"We were planning to go on stage at this great place over in northeast and Jim wasn't coming out of the bathroom. Carlisle knocked but he didn't answer so I just busted in, I was concerned. He was…well he had a needle and his eyes…anyway, he's not OK, I don't know what to do."

I sucked in my breath. I thought about my own secret world. My husband and his nightly trips to the basement, his glazed over eyes and vacant smile. His terrible agitation we both pretended had nothing to do with addiction. "Did he get onstage?" I asked.

"Yes," she said, "he seemed fine after a bit. I was about to drag him to the hospital. But then he snapped out of it and acted like it was nothing. Ben talked to him. I don't know what to do."

I wanted to give her advice, but who was I to help someone with this issue? I could have spoken up here about Ricky, but I didn't want to add to her burden. We talked for minute more and I wished her luck, but I felt I was failing my little sister.

I Will Hunt You Down

I remember the night I discovered I was pregnant with my second son, Perry. I was 2006 and I had brought Pearson to Walla Walla to visit my family. It was my friend Christina's birthday and Pearson was with my parents. My friends Christina and Geri and I were preparing for a night on the town. I had on black jeans and a flowered pink tank top and I felt pretty cute. Heels and fancy hair completed my look of beauty disguising extreme loneliness and desperation. This evening I just couldn't quite muster the energy and exuberance I usually gathered together before a night on the town with my friends. Our usual routine would include cheerful visiting and pre-funking at someone's house while we slathered on makeup and sang to top-forty music then on to The Green Lantern where we would begin our evening. Although I had grown more social that year and usually ended up chatting with a few people in the bar, my number one goal was generally to find and talk to Raymond.

I never will know if Raymond had any idea what he meant to me, and I suppose it is better if he didn't. He was my Ashley Wilkes and, like Scarlett O-Hara I needed someone in my life who wouldn't love me back.

I remember the first time I thought of him again after getting married. I had been married only a few months when I had a vivid dream. In it I was flying through the night sky, over the clouds, when I arrived to my ancestors. They told me I had married the wrong man, that I should have married this guy. They carried me to him and he asked me why I hadn't waited for him. When I woke up I was tremendously sad and had trouble shaking the dream, it had seemed real.

In the past year, Raymond and I had become friends. I guess. It had started when I saw him on my 21st birthday, then I had seen him a couple of months later, at a coffee shop. I was visiting my parents and had walked downtown by myself after Pearson went to sleep. My plan had been to get a cup of peppermint tea, maybe read for a while, and then go home. It was nice to have a minute just to enjoy being on my own without having to worry about my baby and my parents were glad to stay home with him.

But when I walked into Starbucks I saw Raymond. He was by himself, standing at the shelf of mugs. I lit up! I marched up to him, stood right next to him, and said, "So which one are you going to get?"

He looked surprised for a second, but then looked down at me and smiled, "I don't know. It's for my Aunt's birthday."

Before long we decided to take a walk in the snow, leaving Starbucks behind so we could catch up. It was romantic and everything I had ever dreamed of in all my years of thinking about him, we held hands and walked all over town. I was really happy to be with him. I could tell he felt the same way about me and for a couple of hours that night I completely forgot I was married. Though all we did was walk and hold hands, this night affected me for years to come. When he walked me back to my parents house and asked if he could see me again the reality of my life came crashing down on me. I giggled stupidly and said I wished I could, then I went inside.

But I couldn't stop thinking about him. So the next night when my cousins Chester and Loreen invited me out I went, hoping I might see him again. He probably had the same idea, because when I got to the local bar he was already there, seeing me as soon as I walked in the door. I acted overly cheerful and flippant, as if our walk and conversation the night before had meant nothing.

He was sitting a few tables away, his arms crossed, staring at me wearing a somber expression. When I waved cheerfully he only raised his hand, not smiling. He was clearly upset.

"Hey Charlie!" I said, approaching him after awhile.

He didn't smile. "Hi Penny."

"So, how was your day?" I asked him, still grinning and cheerful.

"I talked to my parents. My mom told me you are married."

My smile vanished. I looked at him and saw the pain in his eyes. "Sorry." I said, though I am ashamed to say I didn't probably sound sorry. I was so happy to see him, so excited about being with him, that I just wasn't seeing the big picture of my life.

He lifted his hands in question, like asking me what I was going to do.

"I just want to go to Spain! Or Paris!" I said, still caught up in the glow of sitting near him. Paris? Spain? I don't even know why I came up with this, I was just giddy. Or crazy. Maybe I was so in love with him I went temporarily crazy.

He looked closely at me, maybe trying to see if I was serious.

"I'd go to Spain." He said, smiling for the first time.

And did I grab this opportunity? Did I give him a genuine smile and say, great! Let me hire a lawyer and divorce my unkind and scary husband and then I'll get back to you. Can you wait three months?

No. I didn't do that. Instead I just grinned at him and said, "All right! Fun!"

That's what I did. Then I danced away, joining my cousins. He kept staring at me. I bet he was confused or maybe even mad, I don't know. I was lost and didn't know what to do, so I pretended he didn't matter. But he did matter.

But it didn't end there. From that night on I sought him out every time I was in Walla Walla. I wondered if maybe he looked for me too. We ended up at the same places almost every time I came home. More than a coincidental amount. If I went out with friends or my cousins for a special night, he would eventually appear. When my friend Geri told me he lifted weights at 7:00 in the morning at the Y, I would go to the Y at 7:00 too. We always said hello, never talking about anything important. But if he was around I was unable to focus on anyone or anything else.

Ricky didn't mind how often I would go home to visit my parents. He probably didn't care. And my parents were happy to see Pearson. So for for a few months I thought about Raymond and I like to think Raymond thought about me.

But this didn't last long, just a few months. Ricky and I got pregnant again and my life changed. I lost all interest in traveling to Walla Walla and trying to see Raymond and gladly turned to my newly forming baby. I was content and relieved to finally be free of whatever spell had compelled me to think about this unavailable man.

Three years later I saw him again and we had one last conversation. I was out for a rare night with my friend Christina and we stopped in to a crowded bar to listen to music during the fair. At this point I was divorced and living in Walla Walla. I still thought about Raymond, but getting divorced had been so stressful I hadn't even considered trying to look for him. But on this evening I walked in and right away saw Raymond. He saw me too, and it was as if the previous three years hadn't even happened. Suddenly I was full of energy and life and being out was the funnest thing I could even imagine. I twirled over to him and gave him a big hug, told him how great it was to see him, declared how happy I was for him because I had heard he had just gotten engaged. And then I dashed off, talking to everyone else and not looking at him.

He just stood there, staring at me, watching me ignore him. His fiancé had been a couple of years behind me in school and I had always liked her. She was also there and seemed to be having a fun time. After I had swirled all over, exuberantly greeting old friends, I finally returned to him. I cheerfully said I'd had a dream about him once. He was intensely interested, he pulled me a little ways away, where it was quieter and stared at me, waiting for me to finally say something meaningful. I could see his fiancé standing a few feet away, laughing and talking to friends. I could see the man I had recently started dating, though not seriously, just behind her. He waved at me and smiled.

"Never mind." I said no longer cheerful, now sad and serious, "I shouldn't say this."

He looked earnestly at me, and said, "Are you sure?"

I nodded and he shrugged, his expression almost angry. I apologized and walked away and that is the last private conversation we ever had. A few months later he got married, and and after that when I saw him he wouldn't look me in the eye. Smart man.

But back to the evening I discovered I was pregnant with Perry. I couldn't even bring myself to get excited about the possibility of seeing Raymond, fantasy crush. Even though I looked pretty and it was Saturday night and I had just bought a six-pack of my favorite beer (Newcastle Brown Ale!), I was tired and content to just relax on the couch. My friends encouraged me to have a beer, but when I took a sip it didn't taste good at all, in fact I couldn't even take a swallow. They were concerned, where was fun Penny?

"Here!" Geri said, passing me her glass of red wine, "Try the wine, it's really good."

Again, I took a sip and it was awful! I passed it right back.

"Try mine!" Christina said, pushing her fruity mixed drink toward me. I tried once more, but I couldn't drink this any more than the others.

I decided this was a good time to go relax on the Lay-Z-Boy and next thing I knew I was sound asleep. It wasn't even 9:00.

The next morning my cousin, Loreen just laughed when I told her how I hadn't been able to go out the night before. She encouraged me to go buy a pregnancy test, and when I arrived at her house a little later she was good moral support when the test had that extra plus sign on it. I didn't believe it at first, since Ricky and I hardly even spoke anymore. In fact I made Loreen pee on the other pregnancy test so I could compare a pregnant and non-pregnant stick, and sure enough once I saw the negative next to the positive I knew for sure I was pregnant.

I was so excited! From the moment Perry was even an idea I completely changed. Just as I had been two years earlier as I expected Pearson, I was calm and content and happy. My energy was much slower and more deliberate. I stopped thinking about Raymond. And none of my discontentment seemed to have ever existed.

It took Ricky awhile to adjust to the idea of a second child, but he was pretty great too, right through the whole pregnancy up through the birth. He was even better than he had been with Pearson. When Perry was born he kissed me and said, "Good job, Mom." I thought things would be great, but I was wrong.

Though I have almost nothing but good feelings when I remember back to those baby days, I think this is just a trick that the human mind makes on people to make sure our species doesn't go extinct. Because the reality of the situation was that I have never been more sleep deprived or nervous or stressed out than the first few months my Perry's life. Pearson had been pretty calm, but Perry was colicky, he wanted to nurse almost continuously. But I didn't mind, being a mom was my one saving grace.

And Ricky? Oh, he tried, though he was essentially selfish and inconsiderate for a lot of it. Like when Perry woke in the middle of the night and he yelled from bed for me to, "Shut that baby up." Or when he refused to spend time with us, or eat meals with us. He wasn't a very fun husband, and he hadn't been very helpful with Pearson, but when Perry came along it got much worse.

For awhile I didn't consider my situation to be all too extreme, though I don't think it is fair to downplay it simply because it wasn't bloody. I was married to a man who would fly into unpredictable rages, who called me bitch more than my name, who did not acknowledge me when I spoke, and who threatened me with a knife and a baseball bat. It happened infrequently enough that I simply had little respect for him and wished he would go away, but not often enough that I was aware of how scary a situation I was actually in.

I was enjoying my babies, I felt so lucky to have my sweet baby boy and my fun two year old. I was designing costumes for a play that would be opening in a few months at the community theater. Erica and I were planning an outfit for her to wear to a big concert they would be playing in Seattle, and I often met up with other moms for walks or at the playground. Although I hadn't always wanted to be married to Ricky and he often ignored me when I spoke (I mean literally, as in I would say, "Guess what!" and he wouldn't even turn his head. As if I wasn't in the room. Ouch), I was content with my life. Sure, I was lonely at home because Ricky wouldn't spend time with our family, he wanted to play golf or be in our basement alone. But we were healthy, our home was pretty, and we had plenty of money.

It was about this time that I started taking antidepressants. New mothers often get postpartum depression, and thankfully my mom noticed I was having trouble after Perry was born. Mainly, I wouldn't be able to get out of the house, I felt like everything had to be perfect first. I guess OCD is a good sign that a new mother's brain isn't functioning quite like it should be. Once I started taking a very small dose of medication I really felt like my life was coming together. But it was as though the more content I grew, the more discontent Ricky became. He started coming home from teaching a class or playing golf and grilling me about what I had done during the day, as if to make sure I had done enough to justify my life. As if caring for a two year old and an infant and keeping the house picked up and meals prepared wasn't enough. He wanted me to do larger jobs too, like wash all the windows or reorganize files. I started keeping a list on the white board of the tasks I had completed in the kitchen, but it was never enough. He stopped coming to bed at night, he would stay up until one or two in the morning on his computer. I would beg him to come to bed, to talk to me, but he was unresponsive.

But I was busy and distracted and didn't have time to deal with him. He probably needed an antidepressant too, but I never will figure that out. When he would talk to me he spoke mainly of how he didn't get to play enough golf, how he wasn't getting to fulfill his dream of becoming a professional dancer. His mantra seemed to be, "I never get to do anything I want to do."

He said this throughout the day, whining, about having to be home whenever I asked him to eat dinner with us or accompany us anywhere.

Everything came to a head on November 1, ironic that this is the Day of the Dead, considering I felt like everything we had died that day. It was a beautiful, unnaturally warm day, probably 80 degrees outside, brilliantly sunny and warm.. After taking Pearson to pre-school, I drove with two-month-old Perry to my friend Clara's house and she and her two children and I met up with another friend and her two kids and we walked and walked and walked. It was a such a lovely day that we spent hours just walking around, pushing the strollers through the park then back to Clara's house for tea. It was idyllic, the kind of day that made me so grateful to be a mom.

When I returned home later that afternoon, I made dinner, put Perry down for a nap, put some clothes in the dryer, and picked up some toys. When Ricky came home from teaching a dance class about 4:30, I was in a calm and happy mood, and I greeted him from the kitchen table as he came through the back door from the garage. He did not smile back, he glowered and asked what I did that day. When I said I had gone on a walk with two friends and our kids it made him angry. He stomped through the house and said, "What the F- do you do all day?"

I felt my face grow hot with anger, I stood up and stormed downstairs into the basement and got clothes from the dryer and began stuffing them into the basket. I was doing two and three loads of laundry a day, usually one complete load just for Ricky. It seemed Ricky generated more clothing than the two kids and me put together, and I wondered sometimes if he was simply trying to create work for me. He had other things he did like that too - he would give two-year-old Pearson baskets and boxes of small toys, like those plastic Easter eggs or wooden blocks, then when he dumped them on the floor he would berate me for not picking them up. He made life miserable.

He had followed me downstairs and I started talking talking talking. Because, though I may have been a victim and mistreated, I was never weak or simpering. I can get mad and I can have a harsh tongue, and I started giving him a verbal lashing.

"What do I do all day? Huh? What do I do all day? Obviously nothing, I just sit on my fat butt and do nothing all day because I'm just lazy, that's what I do all day. I'm just a good for nothing! If you didn't spend all of our money playing golf I would hire someone to come over here just to do laundry. How can you wear four outfits a day?"

I was talking furiously, spewing angry words as I grabbed the laundry basket full of clothes to bring upstairs. He followed me into the dining room where I began to fold, angrily punctuating the folds with my monologue. He just stood there, glaring at me, but I didn't really pay attention to him. I was mad, I was mad at him for being a jerk when I was happy and for not appreciating me or our family and for criticizing me every day when staying home with babies is really hard work. I was mad because he would wear a shirt for two hours, with an undershirt and a sweatshirt and throw all three in the dirty clothes and then expect me to wash them even though they weren't dirty.

He yelled, "Shut the F- up!" and held his fist up as if he was going to punch me. I just got angrier.

"Oh yeah? You're going to punch me now? For not doing your laundry fast enough? Ha! Good one!" I wasn't even concerned about him, this is how safe I felt. This is how uninformed and blind I was.

I picked up the laundry basket and stalked into the bedroom to put his stupid clothes away. As I set the basket on the bed I heard the bedroom door slam behind me, I spun around to see what was happening and I knew.

I was in trouble.

Ricky's eyes were cold and dark and murderous, I couldn't even see him in there. I went from indignantly pissed off to hollowly terrified in an instant. Without a word I leaped for the phone. I picked it up and dialed 911, but before it even had a chance to connect he pulled the entire thing from the wall and threw it across the room. Then he came toward me. With both hands, he shoved me backwards, the force throwing me across the room to the floor. He started yelling, but I wasn't hearing his words, I was silent and whimpering. I picked up a floor lamp and made one futile effort to escape, but he easily pulled the lamp from my hands and threw it across the room before shoving me down again. I was on the floor, face down, when he put both knees into my back and has hands around my throat. He was still screaming, and I did hear his words now.

"Die, Bitch! Die!" He kept screaming this over and over as he squeezed harder and tighter around my throat. I got very calm and still here and, though I hadn't been to church very often in the previous years, I started saying the Lord's Prayer to myself in my head as everything started to go black. I said it twice through when I heard, over Ricky's chanting, Perry start to cry.

Ricky let go and got up, going to Perry. I dizzily jumped up and ran after him. Damn if he was going to hurt my baby. But he didn't, he suddenly seemed untroubled. He was looking in at the baby calmly, as if nothing had just happened. I said I should pick him up, he needed to nurse. Ricky let me, and then he even let me take Perry out onto the porch where I said he should sit in the sunshine so he wouldn't get jaundice again. Ricky was quiet, we sat silently for a moment while the baby ate. Then Ricky left me outside and went in. I could hear him inside, freaking out in the bedroom, wailing about what a mess it was. I knew things were still absolutely not ok. I set the baby in the grass and tiptoed just inside the front door and grabbed my car keys, then I dashed out, grabbed Perry, and sprinted to my Suburban. I was just buckling Perry into his seat in the back when Ricky came screaming out of the house, faster than I ever imagined anyone could move toward me. His eyes were crazy. I pulled the vehicle door shut and locked it, jumping through to the driver's seat. The passenger window was open a little way, and Ricky put his fingers in the window and tried to pull it down.

He screamed in, "If you leave me, I will hunt you down and kill you!" and held on to the car as I pulled away. He was still holding onto the side of the Suburban as a Schwan's truck driver pulled toward us, trying to pass. He screamed some obscenities at her, she made eye contact with me and I made the phone sign with my hand and mouthed "Call the police" to her just before pulling away.

Unbelievably, Ricky managed to not only get into his own car and speed to Pearson's preschool and was already there with Pearson when I pulled up, but he had also managed to call my mom and had calmly told her how I had flipped out on him. At the school the teacher leaned in and whispered, "Did he hit you?" Neither one of us wanted to let him take Pearson but he insisted. When he drove off with Pearson I followed, calling my mom at the same time. This is when I learned Ricky had already called her and said I had flown at him for no reason and he was really worried about me. She told me to calm down because if I didn't people would think I was the crazy one, that Ricky sounded totally normal and I was sounding absolutely nuts. I took a few deep breaths and mustered all my acting ability, and by the time I arrived back at my house I at least looked normal.

Thank God Ricky brought Pearson home, it had very much occurred to me that he could take off with him and none of us would see either of them again. But, there they were, on the front porch, to all uninformed observers enjoying a beautiful fall day.

The police arrived a few minutes later, followed by my Uncle Cal, my dad's brother. The police had been called not only by the Schwan's truck driver but also by the preschool. My mom had sent my Uncle Cal over. Being me, my main concern now that my children and I were safe, was to protect my unraveling reputation. I didn't want any of the neighbors to see a police car parked in front of my house. When the police started to question me I glossed over it, claiming most of the responsibility ("Oh, I hadn't gotten the laundry done, I've just been lazy lately, he didn't mean it.") When the police kept referring to a "victim" I didn't know who they were talking about, and I was surprised when I asked and they told me it was me. I was the victim.

It took me a few days to acknowledge that I was in a bad situation and needed to leave. Thank goodness for the educated and respectful police officers who not only informed me that I was a victim of domestic abuse and that I needed to get out or it most certainly would escalate, but who also returned to my house later to tell me again how important it was for me to leave the bad situation as well as to give me the phone number of the domestic abuse line at the YWCA. The YWCA was also very helpful, and it was the counsellor there who gave me the truest understanding of why I needed to leave.

"Do you want you sons to grow up to be abused?" She asked me that night when I called the number.

"No!" I practically shouted.

"Do you want your sons to be abusers?"

"Of course not!"

"This is what will happen if you stay with a man who abuses you. Your children will think it is ok for people to treat each other this way. The only way to break the cycle is to walk away."

So, even though it was extremely difficult, I left. I left my beautiful home and comfortable life and hid out in my parent's house in Walla Walla. I endured people gossiping about me, expressing deep interest only to never speak to me again after hearing my story. Many of the nice mom-friends I had met in LA never spoke to me again. I lost a lot of money. I was so scared he would hold true to his promise of hunting me down and killing me that I didn't sleep well for nearly a year. I have never been skinnier or more nervous.

But with time things evened out. Ricky eventually managed to get his life in order well enough where the kids could go visit with him, though I never trusted him to be free of drugs and always made sure his mom would be around. Ricky stayed in Los Angeles and lived with his mother. She was as worried about him as I was and she and I always maintained a good relationship, so twice a year I would bring the kids up to stay with her and they always loved seeing their dad. I always encouraged a good relationship and they love him and enjoy being with him.

It wasn't an easy time at first, but I lived with my parents in their beautiful home and they gave me the stability we needed for a good life. And though men made me extremely uncomfortable for a long time, I dated on occasion.

I wonder sometimes what the purpose of all that ever was, if that great big mess that was my marriage has anything positive to offer the world. Of course, my kids, yes. But the other part, the nearly 3 years of marriage part. Will I ever be able to look back and just remember the good? The silly word games we would play, trips to the beach, sharing the newspaper over breakfast in the morning? It's such a shame that our last fiery day together overwhelms the other years we were together. I hope some day that bad afternoon can fade further into the recesses of my mind leaving me with happier memories of my marriage.

Erica felt terrible for not noticing. Everyone did, but I assured them that I had hid it from them, I had tried so hard to keep them from worrying that it hadn't occurred to me that I wasn't doing the right thing. After Ricky took off, Erica would get really upset if she ever heard that Jim was spending time with him. Jim and Ricky had been good friends, since their Kids Rock days. There wasn't much Erica could do about them spending time together.

Roxana

The funny thing was, once Ricky returned to Los Angeles his life took off. He met up with Roxana almost immediately, so quickly in fact I had to accept that they had probably always had something going on. But I was so glad he was gone and we were safe. I was just glad he had someone to keep him distracted.

When he first met Roxana they had worked together on Kids Rock. Erica hadn't even known they dated, they hardly spoke to each other. Roxana was uniformly friendly and at the same time unkind to everyone. She was completely untrustworthy and her relationship with Ricky was a complete surprise to everyone. It wasn't until much later that I started to piece together how they must have snuck out after filming to shoot up. When we were married I never could get Ricky to give me much of a backstory and really I didn't much want to hear it. Roxana was one of those girls I just couldn't stand hearing about. Any time anyone mentioned her name around me I would just imagine her big loopy letters proclaiming her love for my husband and I would feel sick.

But after Ricky returned to Los Angeles he immediately started spending time with Roxana again, a fact I would't even have known about except for about this same time The Flying Foes started getting really big and they signed with Big Band

Records. It was 2007 and Erica, Ben, Carlisle and Jim were now living in LA and were playing bigger and bigger venues each time Erica and I spoke on the phone.

Only one month after I ran away from him, she called me, concerned. "Ricky was here." She told me as I answered.

"Not looking for me I hope," was my instant response.

"No, not at all, in fact he hardly even acknowledged that he had been my brother-in-law for three years. God, I hate that guy. I couldn't even be in the club after they showed up, I got Angie to take me home. We had just played the best show, you should have seen how many people were here. And they knew our music, it was great! But then Ricky showed up with Roxana, remember her? She was as evil as ever, pretending we were friendly and then telling me how terribly I'd done. All under the guise of friendship, of course."

"Of course." I said, I was familiar with Roxana's subtle jabs.

I shook my head, looking out at Perry and Pearson who were happily running around my parents living room. "I always just tried to avoid her. Plus heard how fabulous she was from people who didn't know better."

"I guess. If you can call a super skinny, hollow-eyed junkie fabulous. She just sat there, her mouth kind of half open and staring at nothing like she was totally bored. I was so annoyed she was there. And Ricky was all charming and smiling and acting like we were all friends, giving the guys high fives. They all bought it too, I was pissed at them. I can't believe they were even talking to them."

I was surprised to hear Erica so emotional about the issue. Usually she only noticed people she liked. But Roxana had always managed to make her feel terrible. Now she managed to make both of us feel terrible. I had to change the subject.

"Angie? You hired her again?" I said, latching onto that one small sentence she had thrown out there.

"Yes, isn't that great? I can't believe she's available, I thought she'd work for Simone forever but I guess models are too demanding for our girl Angie!"

Angie and her daughter had both helped our family while Erica was working on Kids Rock. Angelica Flores had worked as Erica's assistant for her entire run on the show and she and her daughter, Samantha, had been a rock for our entire family. I was really glad to hear she was back in the picture.

After this I started seeing Ricky and Roxana pictured on all the LA blogs and photogs, he became famous for being famous. His only real talent was in being in the right place at the right time wearing the right clothes posing with the right people. His cool, dark looks and green eyes along with her beautiful angry glare were a benefit to any stylized photo. I tried not to pay any attention, I was just thankful to be getting on with my own life.

Flying Foes: L.A

Getting divorced at 22, with two tiny children, is not easy. In fact, I strongly suspect getting divorced is never easy for anyone. But having my mother around to help me, living in a beautiful home in a pretty, kid-friendly town was pleasant and time passed quickly. Sure, there were days when I would have done anything for a break, when my mom was so engrossed by whatever decorating project or dinner party she had thrown herself into and I had no one to really talk to about my boys. Or when I would take them to a school event and I was the only single mom, the only one trying frantically to run around after two kids at the same time while many moms sat and calmly visited while their single child played happily with their husband.

It was after an open house at the preschool when I spent the entire event chasing two year old Perry around the playground and missed the whole teacher presentation that I hired a professional nanny. Finding Isabel was a stroke of luck and I made sure to treat her very well - a great salary, bonuses, giving her a beautiful space to live in. She had just graduated from the state university with a degree in elementary education and had wanted to return to Walla Walla to teach, but I snagged her instead. She was the granddaughter of my mom's massage therapist, very calm and patient. I paid her $15,000 more a year than any of the teachers in town, plus gave her plenty of free time and took her with us on our frequent trips to Los Angeles. She had the cute apartment above the garage and we all loved her.

The boys and I had so much fun, I used to wonder how life would have been different if Ricky had stuck around. I don't think I would have been able to give my kids the calm and fun if their dad had been there making things uncomfortable. Even though the divorced was a stigma for all of us, it was also freeing because it gave me the freedom to do what I thought was best.

Pearson and Perry saw Ricky, though rarely on his own; his family would always be around, eager to spend time with the boys too. Because Erica and The Flying Foes were so successful, we spent a lot of time in Los Angeles. I helped them much more with costumes and stage design than I ever imagined I would help anyone when I first studied at UCLA.

For each new show, Erica and the guys would usually come up with an overarching theme and we would branch out from there. One of their first shows in LA was at a smaller venue called Emblem in an up and coming industrial area. We covered the concrete stage with small white lights and shiny tinsel and brought in a fog machine to create a haunting scene for their Graveyard themed October show.

By spring of 2007 in Los Angeles they were ready to kick off a big tour starting with an enormous, sold-out show at Lovelace Music Hall. That first year in LA had been so successful that Big Band Records was pulling out all the stops. They had an enormous tour bus parked out behind The Lovelace and right after their show they would be heading out on a 100 city tour. They had just released their first big label record and they had three songs climbing up the chart. Two of them, "My

Heart" and "Stink Eye" were competing with each other for number one song. The Flying Foes were on their way.

My parents, the kids, Isabel and I spent a week with Erica helping her prepare for the kick-off show. Well, my dad and I helped while Isabel took the kids to museums and playgrounds and my mom paced around fretting. My dad was constantly on the phone barking out instructions to promoters and handlers. Between him and Big Band Records this was one of the most well-publicized tours in history. Erica and Jim had given up trying to get him to tone it down, they figured they could now rest assured at having established themselves through talent rather than through their parental connections. Jim's own parents were making appearances all over town, waving and giving speeches to magazines and TV crews about the upcoming show and tour, it was a madhouse and the people were loving it.

We were staying with Erica who had set up residence in my parents' Hollywood Hills mansion. I spent most of my days taking care of last minute details for the Midsummer Night's Dream themed stage and costume design. Fairies and wood-elves would be sharing the stage with Erica and her mostly black-clad band. We had drop-down elevators sneaking her off to other parts of the stage with fire and smoke concealing costume changes. This was by far our biggest production and Erica's passion and enthusiasm was contagious.

The show and the tour were amazing, the crowds loved the Foes, Erica, all of them. Erica was everyone's sweetheart, always cheerful and enthusiastic. Ben was so steady and solid, he had his own brand of follower, usually consisting of bespectacled teenaged girls. Carlisle kept to himself, he was hard for photographers to pin down. But with his signature black jacket and long dark hair and long-legged strut, he could never hide for long. He tended to just stay in hiding. It was lucky he enjoyed being by himself and only going out at night, because he really didn't like the crowds. He was the only one who stayed single too. Ben was comfortably settled in with Jenna while Jim's hair stylist, Kelly, had joined them in LA.

Jim was the heartthrob, he had girls throwing their bras at him while he was on stage, screaming they wanted his baby, practically attacking him if they saw him in public. I would have hated it, but he was used to it. Poor Jim, really, he just laughed it all off and seemed really centered about it, but he never really got any peace.

I asked Erica if he was clean, if she suspected he was still using heroine or anything. She looked downcast, this was the thorn in their side. He still disappeared at times, grew distant, had an inexplicable temper no one could explain. But when they asked him he just laughed, said not to worry. So she said they had decided not to, everything else was going so well.

They had to hire a young guy and then later a team just to take care of fan mail. George was great, he went to the Post Office every day, brought home the huge bags, and he and this group of people would send out chatty letters and signed photos to all the fans. Plus they had to hire another team just to maintain all the social media.

I loved listening to her describe the latest concert or photo shoot. After their first tour they came back so popular I couldn't turn on the radio in my car without hearing one of their catchy songs. Their pictures were all over the magazines in the grocery store, and every few weeks a reporter would call our house just to interview mom or dad or me about Erica. It was crazy.

For the next couple of years The Flying Foes spent half the year on tour. If we didn't join Erica somewhere along the way we would never see her since they were traveling all over the US and later all over the world. The kids enjoyed all of it, having a famous aunt was pretty cool.

Both boys shared Aunt Erica's love for music, though Pearson was more passionate about the guitar than in singing while Perry was starting to make up lyrics and rhymes. We all had fun joining her at concerts, though we were happiest when she came home and just relaxed with us as a family. In 2012, when the boys were six and eight, Erica came for Christmas and I asked her if she ever felt like settling down.

"No way! Never!" She laughed, leaning back against the pillow of her bed. But I saw something in her eyes that made me wonder if maybe she really did want to settle down.

We were in her room at our parents house, she had the rounded corner room overlooking our backyard. When my mom had begun to worry about her never buying her own house she had insisted she redecorate her own bedroom in their house. But Erica had recently bought a comfortable ranch-style house in the hills, near our parents LA house. I suspected this might be the first sign she was ready to spend more time at home.

"But what about marriage? Babies? You won't be young forever you know." I said.

At 28 I was beginning to see all my friends from school have babies. I had my own two and didn't think I needed to have more, but I didn't want to see my little sister miss out on the opportunity if she wanted it.

She looked off, wistfully, "Yeah, I always wanted a kid or two. But not in LA, it's too crowded and materialistic. I want to do it like you have, quiet and laid back, let them ride their bikes to a friend's house and not have to worry, join the stroller brigade. But not yet! Give me a few more years. Besides, maybe Malcolm will end up being The One!"

I raised my eyebrows, wondering if something had changed. She rarely mentioned this guy Malcolm. He was some big shot Hollywood guy, but he didn't seem very committed.

"What about….Charlie Jones?" I asked her. "I saw Amanda at our book club last week."

The effect was immediate. Her eyes widened and the look of hope that crossed her face surprised me.

"You haven't forgotten him, have you?" I was surprised, though not entirely. Even though he was married now, I hadn't ever really forgotten Raymond either. There is something about that first love.

"I looked him up not too long ago," she said, I could tell she was embarrassed because she was shaking her head and rubbing her forehead. "He's married. He married this really cute girl and they look happy. I totally stalked his Facebook, they have a great-looking dog."

"Well, that's life. You know there is not just one guy out there." I told her, maybe trying to convince myself more than her. "Meet someone. Do the online dating thing."

We got a huge laugh out of that. Imagine what a guy would think if he showed up at a blind date - and it was Erica Princeton!

"But really, choose someone, E. You're a catch, lady. If you want somebody, let him know."

She nodded thoughtfully. Then pinpointed her gaze at me.

"And what about you!" She asked gleefully. "Here you are so convinced my life will only be complete once I have some dude telling me what to do. What about you? Where's your guy, huh?"

I laughed, shaking my head. I had a guy I had been dating for years, but he was so frustrating I didn't even want to mention him to my sister. It was going absolutely no where and I was beginning to wonder if maybe that was all I could really handle.

"Oh, I date," was all I could mumble out, "just no one special."

"Pen, you have got to get over your fear of men. Or whatever it is, tell me about this guy. What do you mean you are dating someone?"

So I spilled my guts about Brian Murphy.

Moving On

Getting divorced had only taken three months. It is amazing how quickly and inexpensively people can divorce if there is not an argument, and Ricky definitely could not give me an argument. I started piecing my life back together, but realized quickly my life was now completely different. I'm not sure how it is for other people, but getting divorced caused me to lose many other relationships than just my husband. I was no longer a wife, so I no longer fit into that social realm. I was no longer included in events with other couples, something that hurt briefly. But I eventually developed new friendships.

My book club was one group that really saved me. My friends Geri, Amanda, and I started it and we have been meeting monthly ever since I came back to town. Though I use the term 'we' loosely because only three of us were in the original book club, Geri, Amanda, and me. A few of our friends have moved away. Heather moved to Africa. Jane is back East. Erica is in Portland. Allison is in Seattle. Nicole moved to Portland. Other ladies have come and gone over the years, some stay longer than others, but the club itself remains intact and it has sustained me all these years.

We joke, as many ladies' book clubs do, that we are actually a wine club that reads and discusses books on occasion. Because we usually spend the first hour or two just catching up, and if we get to the book, great. It was at one of these book club meetings, about a year after I had left Ricky, that I finally told my friends I was thinking of dating again. They were delighted, mainly because for the past year any time anyone brought it up I would get very upset and say I would never go out with a man again, all men not in my immediate family scared me.

For the first year after I was on my own I was so afraid of men, any unknown man, that if I found myself alone with a man I would instantly bolt for the nearest door. I didn't care what anybody thought, I didn't trust half the world's population and there was nothing anyone could say to help me. But I went to a counsellor once a week and she helped me get calm, I read anything I could about overcoming trauma, I practiced yoga, I went to Jazzercise. I did everything I could to heal. And eventually I felt like I might be ready to trust again. Maybe.

Everyone had a suggestion for me, but I had already decided who I had my sights set on, a quiet guy who worked at my kids' preschool named Craig. Craig seemed like a good choice for a first venture out in the dating world mainly because I could trust him. I'd gone to school with him since the seventh grade and I had seen around the pre-school, he seemed pretty safe. Of course, we had no chemistry and little in common, so when I asked him out for coffee it never went any further than about half hour of kid-related conversation, but hey! I was on my way to the world of dating.

Once I entered the dating world my family and friends all had someone in mind, but I was pretty hesitant. But one name kept coming up from all different people: Brian Murphy. My mom suggested him, she had hired him to re-landscape the front yard, she said he was friendly. My friend Donna from yoga and her husband Doug were friends with him, they mentioned how his wife had left him and how nice he was. But what really decided it for me was that his older brother Danny was my accountant and I felt safe with him. I figured if Danny wasn't too scary then Brian probably wouldn't be either. I decided to give him a call.

So the day after Christmas I got my kids, at this point 1 and 3, settled in front of a cartoon and called this Brian guy. Right away we could talk, he was funny and polite and after about twenty minutes he asked if I would like to have diner with him. At first I was really eager about him, he seemed so perfect. Thank God Brian didn't reciprocate my feelings and kept sensibly telling me he wasn't ready, he really liked me but he wasn't sure if we were right for each other, he needed space, etc. He had managed to keep me at arms length while still taking me on weekly dates for four entire years, something I could look at as either terrible or wonderful, depending on what I wanted out of life. I was grateful to Brian for being a polite and respectful guy to date while I learned how to trust men again. Not to mention, my kids never had to deal with the trauma of having strange men in and out or an intrusive boyfriend since Brian was the type who would meet me at the door and wave at the children before taking me to dinner. Even though it felt frustrating, dating a noncommittal man like this was about all I could handle after such a difficult marriage and divorce.

That night when I told Erica all about Brian Murphy, describing how we never had committed to anything more than just weekly dates. She was appalled.

"Do you love this guy?" She had asked me.

"Well…no." I admitted, looking at the floor. We were still in her room in our parent's house, though by this point we had popped popcorn and were both laying on her fluffy white bed. Christmas Eve was the next day and we had a ton to do to prepare, but we had so much to talk about we didn't even care that it was almost two in the morning.

"Dump him Sis! He's a drip! You deserve so much better than this guy. Mom said she had fixed you up with some landscape dude years ago, but you never said anything about it. I had no idea this had dragged on so long."

I laughed, "What! Who are you to give this advice! How long have you been dating that Malcolm guy?"

She blushed, "Well, yeah, a year. A year too long…but exactly. That's what I mean. I had no idea you had a noncommittal guy too."

"I wouldn't exactly call him noncommittal," I told her, "that would imply I want a commitment. He's just happy to go out every once in awhile, as am I. I suppose."

"You suppose? How long are you going to be alone? Don't you want to ever have a serious guy in your life again?" She asked me, her look of concern so genuine it caught me off guard.

I thought about it for awhile and decided she was right. Brian was safe. I didn't know if he dated other girls, and I imagined it was certainly possible. He wouldn't even know if I was going out with other people, though I decided it would be polite to tell him if I were.

So I brought up the subject at our next Friday night date, after the Christmas holiday. He seemed surprised.

"I thought we were good. Why would you want to date other people?" He asked me, looking genuinely surprised.

"I'm just ready for more, Brian, I've been single for a long time now and I realize maybe I might need a genuine relationship. You know, someone who eventually wants to live together, maybe get married."

He looked sadly down at his steak, I had ruined his night. The only thing he really seemed to be concerned about was enjoying a good dinner, maybe a couple of heavy metal songs at the bar, and here I was tossing this bomb on him. He shook his head, and looked up at me.

"I'm sure you will make someone a good wife someday," he said, his brown eyes thoughtful, "but I really need someone who doesn't have kids. Someone who shares my political beliefs. You know this."

I sighed. I did know this. It wasn't as if I had never ventured to have this conversation before, but I had always endured the brick wall. And passively agreed to see him again after he basically told me I wasn't good enough to marry, just good enough to hang out with on occasion.

"I'm sorry she hasn't walked into your life yet Brian. Let me do you a favor. And myself too," I said with a conviction I hadn't felt in a long time. Maybe Erica was right, maybe I was ready for more! "But neither one of us will never find that special someone if we are wasting our time on each other. Take care." And with that, I tossed some money on the table for my share of my uneaten dinner and I walked out, my head held high.

Sadly for Brian, when I finally decided I wanted to move on and make room for a relationship with someone who wanted something more than a dinner date and an occasional evening out to hear some music he decided he might have wanted to get married after all. I ran into him a few months later. I was out with Geri and Amanda, we were visiting at one of my favorite downtown places, when my two friends got pained expressions on their faces.

"What?" I looked behind me, toward the direction of their eyes.

There was Brian, standing just a few feet away. He was forlornly looking at me, managing a brave smile. I was completely over his nonsense. I smiled brightly and greeted him before turning back to my friends.

He approached our table, "Can we talk?" he asked me sadly.

"Sure," I said, not moving. "What's up?" I maintained a cheerful indifference.

He looked at my friends, who were thrilled at my dismissal of this years-long time waster, then back at me. I knew he wanted me to go on a walk with him, we had done this before, over and over for four years. I would abandon my fun evening, join him for a walk, listen to all the reasons he missed me and the near-promises of commitment…and within three months I'd be back to miserably seeing him once a week, unable to get him to agree to even a family event or a vacation. No way.

I held my ground, looking up at him and smiling. "What's going on Brian? Are you having a good night?"

Realizing I was done with the on again/off again game and was not going to speak to him privately, he sighed and shook his head, "No, not really. It's lonely without you."

Geri stifled a laugh, though Brian was too intent on getting me to feel sorry for him to notice her.

I shook my head, tsk-tsking sympathetically. "Yeah, it can be hard. You'll be fine, a nice guy like you." I was just about to wish him luck when a cute older brunette joined him, putting her arm proprietarily through his.

"Bri, are you going to come sit down?" She asked him while giving me a hard look.

"What? Oh, yeah. Be right there." With one final pathetic hound dog look back at me he followed her to a table where two other couples sat looking at us. I smiled and nodded at his friends who waved slightly. I'm sure they were as happy as my own friends that we were through.

My friends and I dissolved into giggles, "What a jerk!" Geri laughed, "I can't believe he is on a date with some other poor girl and at the same time pining away over you. He got what he deserves."

Amanda nodded, "Yeah, good job Pen, you are so much better off without that guy."

I had to agree. People like this usually just end up alone, I'm not sure what they are afraid of, but I can venture to guess. Commitment and marriage and connection come with enormous risk. Being alone can be much easier.

Ricky and Roxana Crash the Party

2014

Ricky and Roxana. Here, at their 10th Anniversary Concert!
I couldn't believe my ex-husband had the gall to bring his
girlfriend backstage at The Flying Foes Los Angeles concert. I
looked at Erica, whose relaxed, after-a-great-show expression
had hardened at Ricky's uninvited entrance.

"Great show you guys!" Ricky called out cheerfully, his
handsome face lighting up in a nearly-sincere smile. If I hadn't
been married to him long ago I would have thought he was
charming. Now I know that half of what he says is just hollow,
the other half is designed to make people do something for his
benefit.

"Jim!" Ricky strode over and gave Jim a big hug, "I have a
gift for you my man."

I was annoyed he had burst in, but Erica looked really
concerned. I wondered what kind of gift Ricky had for Jim.

"Excuse me," I muttered, going quickly into the bathroom so
I didn't have to watch my ex-husband try to charm my sister and
her band.

Sure, I saw him every so often when our kids visited, but he
generally managed to avoid situations where he would see me
socially. My family and friends were even more disgusted with

him than me, mainly because they had to deal with my sadness
for years after he failed us. But to see him here was too much.
This was my sister's big night, a huge concert, and our entire
family was here. Even our boys had joined us, though their dad
hadn't mentioned to them he would be here. I wondered if he
had seen them with my parents before he came backstage.

Roxana had still held her signature hollowed-eyed look,
though now that she was nearing thirty it didn't make her look
cool as much as vacant and unintelligent. The couple of seconds
I had been in the same room with them I had looked at both my
ex-husband and his new wife, expecting her to acknowledge me.
But she didn't even let her eyes rest on me, it was as if I wasn't
there. In all the years I had known her Roxana had never once
spoken to me. When Ricky and I met up to exchange the kids
when they were younger, she did not accompany him and now
that they were older if we were ever at the same function - a
game or concert or ceremony, Roxana was always conveniently
busy.

I never minded, I have no delusions about being friends with
her, but it makes it so much more awkward that she won't even
acknowledge my existence. I had to shrug it off, chalking it up
to either A) her feelings of guilt for cheating with him while we
were married, B) her feelings of guilt for always being terrible to
my sister, or C) a fifteen year drug habit that addled her brain. It
was probably a combination, but she wasn't someone I had a
desire to know anyway.

No matter how I felt about my ex or his current wife, I didn't
want them to think I didn't have a good life. I took a few
moments to pull some lipstick out of my purse and add it to my
cheeks and my lips. At least I could look my best, I thought,
smiling at myself in the mirror. Being 30 was better than I had
thought it would be. I had great energy and my skin looked

healthy. I felt pretty good as I walked out of the bathroom, my head held high.

When I emerged only Ben and Carlisle were in the lounge. "Where did Jim and Erica go?" I asked Ben, who was standing closest to me.

Ben rolled his eyes, "Erica left right after you, she wants to go out on the town. But Jim? I can't believe that dud. Jim just left with Ricky and Roxana. He said he'd 'be right back.'" Ben held up air quotes as he imitated Jim. Obviously he didn't expect Jim to return any time soon.

I shook my head, "I don't see what the draw is."

Carlisle, who was pulling on different boots nearby, interjected. "I do."

"What?" I asked, "What do you mean?"

"I see the draw." Carlisle finished lacing his boots and stood up, pulling on his leather jacket.

"It's the H. Jim's still on it, or he got back on it. Or whatever. Don't talk about it to Kelly, she just yells at him and it makes it worse. He hides out, doesn't get help. She'll figure out pretty quick that he's gone and I don't plan on being around to deal with that shitshow."

I looked at Ben. "Is this true?" Ben nodded sadly.

"Don't worry Penny, he'll be fine." Carlisle said, unconcerned. "He'll be gone for a few days with your gem of an ex-husband, he'll return all tired and beaten down. He may decide to go relax in rehab for a few weeks…he'll be fine. We're used to it."

I didn't feel like it was fine, but Carlisle and Ben were so blasé about it I decided to just ignore it like they were doing. Jim was an adult, what could I do? Besides, my sons' dad was out there doing the same thing. Trying to swallow past the anxious lump in my throat, I went to Erica's dressing room to find her. She was just shimmying into a stretchy, off-the-shoulder black dress when I walked in. Dabbing on some lipstick and fluffing out her blonde hair she smiled at me.

"OK! Let's go out and party like rock stars! Where's Jim? He didn't leave with Ricky, right? I told them not to take him anywhere, your ex is bad news." She was full of exuberant energy, wiggling around in a little dance. Normally I would have been glad to be a part of it, but tonight I was the barer of bad news.

"Jim already left." I said, hoping she wouldn't ask any more.

"Left? What do you mean?" Her eyes narrowed. "Do you mean with Ricky and Roxana?"

I nodded.

"Those scumbags!" She exploded. "I'm telling Kelly."

She pushed past me into the hall and called out to Jim's wife who immediately came out of Jim's dressing room.

"I know!" Kelly said, indignant. "Seriously, should I just leave him Erica? He promised."

Erica shook her head, "Kelly you know you don't mean that. Let's go track him down. Maybe we can talk some sense into him before he does anything stupid."

She turned to me, "Did they say where they were going?"

I shook my head, "No, I took one look at Roxana and hid in the bathroom. I just didn't have it in me to deal with her, I should get over this by now, huh? But let's go ask Ben or Carlisle."

Both Ben and Carlisle directed us to The Fountain, the newest night club to open downtown.

Carlisle rolled his eyes, "You know the Rhodes will go there since the most photographers will be there."

"Yeah, everyone'll be going crazy once Jim walks in." Ben added, "should we go add to the fray? Erica, you down?"

Carlisle laughed, "Count me out, I can't stand the screaming. I wish I could just meet a girl who doesn't know I'm famous."

Erica was still agitated, "Don't you guys see how lame this is! Ricky's going to get him all hooked on smack again and we'll have to deal with it for the next month until he goes to rehab then we can't even finish out our tour. Remember last time?"

Ben and Carlisle finally got it, "Ugh," said Carlisle, hauling himself out of the chair he was comfortably splayed across, "I see your point. OK, I'm there."

The Fountain

The Fountain was hopping, we could see the crowd spilling out over the sidewalk as soon as their limo turned the corner. When we pulled up to the curb we followed Erica to the entrance. She was so used to being famous that it didn't even faze her that every single person there grew almost silent as she strode by. The crowd parted for her, allowing her to walk right up to the doorman. Other people had probably been standing out front in their nicest clothes since the sun set, but Erica just walked right up and didn't even think about whether or not she'd get in.

The doorman kept an impressively impassive face as he lifted the red velvet rope for her to pass through, she thanked him and pointed out Kelly, Ben, Jenna, Carlisle, and me before plunging through the glass doors. Thank God she had thought of that! One of our first times going into a club with a large group she hadn't considered the fact that other people weren't extraordinarily famous, rich, and beautiful like her and had disappeared into the club without me, Jenna, and Carlisle. The three of us had stood around outside with the rest of the crowd for ten minutes after everyone else slipped past the rope without us. The doorman didn't recognize Carlisle, and Jenna and I were nobodies, so he hadn't let us in. Erica had finally realized we weren't there and had come back out to retrieve us, good thing too because we were seconds away from calling a cab and going home.

Once inside I surveyed the club, impressed it was not the usual cement and strobe light but instead was an imitation of an elegant mansion complete with a curving staircase, opulent chandelier, and plush oriental rugs. There was less of a crowd inside and the elegant people scattered around were trying to appear disinterested in Erica Princeton and her band coming through the door. Erica scanned the room, looking for Jim, but none of us saw him. Ben was the first to see Ricky and Roxana, lounging lazily against a strategically-placed table at the back.

Erica marched toward them. "Where's Jim?" She snapped in an uncharacteristically rude tone.

Ricky looked up at her through hooded eyes that didn't quite focus. Roxana didn't even move her eyes from the mid-distant point she was intent upon.

"Oh hey Erica, great show." He drawled.

"You already told me that!" She snapped. "Where's Jim?"

"Jim? Oh I think he's still in the loo." Ricky said with a bored head nod toward the row of bathrooms on the other side of the room.

Erica looked at Kelly who clenched her jaw, shaking her head. Kelly was clearly pissed. I imagined she was fed up with dealing with Jim's addiction. I understood, after awhile all you can do is just wait for a person to figure it out for themselves. Ben and Carlisle didn't seem eager to go in after Jim, either. The Flying Foes had a three month tour stretched in front of them, the last thing they needed was for Jim to go spiraling down on a bender.

With a shrug, Erica looked at us and said, "I'm just going to go get him. We've got another show in two days." Before marching off in the direction of the bathrooms. I followed behind, not sure if she might need help. I remembered my own experiences trying to entice Ricky to stay clean had never gone very well.

When she reached the men's bathroom, she walked right in. No one seemed too surprised to see two woman entering the men's room, though once guys realized one of the women was Erica Princeton they showed a lot more interest. She looked under the stalls and, spotting Jim's black Converse, knocked on the door.

"Jim? I need you to come home with me. Kelly's out in the club. It doesn't matter what you've already done or whatever, but we've got to go." He didn't answer.

She looked at me and rolled her eyes, holding up her hands and mouthing 'seriously?'

Using her fingernail to turn the circular latch, she pushed the door open, her brow creased in concern. I looked at the guys in the bathroom, none actually going to the bathroom now, all just watching this drama unfold in front of them.

"Jim? Jim?" As she pushed open the bathroom door I heard her gasp, I looked over her shoulder and the first thing I saw was the top of Jim's head, his body hunched over. His sleeve was rolled up to reveal his forearm, a hypodermic needle stuck in his vein. Erica began shaking her head, willing this to not be happening. But it was happening. Before she had a chance to make a sound Kelly was behind us, trying to see over my shoulder.

"What is it? Why isn't he coming out? What's going on?" Kelly's voice betrayed her panic. Her bright blue eyelids, a few moments before so beautiful, were now garish against her suddenly pale skin.

Erica and Kelly knew what had happened, they knew immediately that Ricky and Roxana were not just there to visit and that their gift for Jim was more than just a gift. It was heroin and Jim had not been prepared for the strength of the drug.

As Kelly crouched over her husband she let out a low wail that I could hear as I bolted back out through the club and onto the sidewalk. I ran, punching keys on my cell phone, frantically dialing 911. News of the tragedy sped through the crowded club, first trickling to the rest of the band, Ricky and Roxana, and then sprinkling like poison out to the everybody else. It was a horrible drama that would be replayed over and over, for days and weeks, all over the media. Jim Jackson, guitarist for Flying Foes, overdoses on heroin in the bathroom of a dance club while Erica Princeton looks on. From the speculation to his drug background to the details of his last few minutes and subsequent failed resuscitation, the sudden death of Jim Jackson forever altered more lives than just his own.

As the ambulance pulled away from the back door, Erica and I watched while waiting for the limo, the crowd giving us a wide berth. We stood in complete darkness, even in our grief we were aware of the media and were doing everything we could to keep the million amateur journalists around us from getting any clear pictures. Carlisle and Ben stood on either side of us, equally distraught. Ricky and Roxana had immediately disappeared.

"Man, how'd he get hooked up again with that garbage?" Carlisle sighed, shaking his head. Though his appearance might suggest otherwise, Carlisle had been raised in a conservative family and had never done more than drink an occasional glass of champagne at a celebration. He had never understood Jim's penchant for wildness. Though being a good friend had quietly accepted him when he was ready to crawl back from whatever bender he'd been on.

Erica, slumping against the backdoor of the club couldn't even answer, her grief and shock were too great. A great commotion behind us erupted as Angelica, Erica's assistant, came forcefully through the backdoor. We were all relieved at her take-charge attitude, and when a few minutes later the limo pulled up we readily followed her command to get in.

Aftermath

"You need air Erica," Angie said as we sped off in the limo, "breathe."

Before Erica had a chance to resist, Angie had pulled her delicate frame into a big bear hug. By the time the town car pulled out onto the highway Angie was forcing us to all drink water and eat some quiche

Angie directed the driver to Erica's Hollywood Hills Ranch Style home, punching the gate key purposefully and guiding the driver through the gate. Clicking the security code automatically, Erica and Angie led us inside, I paused momentarily to admire my sister's lovely home before dragging myself upstairs. Angie had lived with Erica since she had bought her new house. Our whole family was grateful for the steady solidity of Angie, thankful Erica was able to rely on such a capable assistant to care for her even when she and the band were traveling. Were traveling.

Again the realization that Jim was gone hit, Erica shook her head and sank to her knees in tears. Angie patted her shoulder, cooing soothingly as Erica cried. Ben, Jenna, Carlisle, and I were brushing tears away too. I hated to think of what Kelly was going through, traveling in the ambulance and at the hospital.

"Angie, should we call Kelly? Do you think she needs help at the hospital?"

Angie nodded, "She's going to need all the help we can give her. Not just emotional, but to keep those damn picture-takers away too. I already called Joe, a manager is good at getting the right spin on a story. Plus he'll get Kelly out of there. But you all need to see her and give her support. We'll make a plan. For now, though, let's try to get some sleep."

Nobody wanted to leave, Jenna and Ben took the downstairs guest room and Carlisle headed up to the smaller second floor suite. I decided I'd stay with Erica. Angie's directions were soothing and I just numbly followed her lead.

Angie had always known just what to do. When Erica had first grown famous on the 'Kids Rock' program 15 years earlier Angie had worked as a wardrobe assistant, a seamstress assigned to fix buttons, launder costumes, and make sure the teenage cast of the popular television show never had costumes that looked worn or dirty. One low afternoon Roxana Shilling had taken her subtle jabs too far. Erica had been hiding her tears in the middle of a rack of clothes. This is where she was when Angie had found her and befriended her with her straightforward, in-command personality.

Though our mother, the world-wide loved Adelaide Princeton, was kind and fun, her propensity to sudden breakdowns or raging fits made growing up with her anxiety-provoking. Angelica Flores, oldest of five siblings, mother to three children, was a blessing to our family. Not only did Erica grow to rely on her clear decision-making, so did the rest of us. It was soothing to be able to have someone mother us after so many years of Adelaide who considered her most important mothering skill to be getting us invited to the right party or making sure we vacationed in the most happening hot-spot. Angie gave our family balance.

And this night, balance was something we all greatly needed. Once we were in her room, showered and wrapped in fluffy robes, Erica really broke down. Her sobs left me feeling helpless. But I did the best I could, patting her back soothingly as Angie had, my own tears sliding easily down my cheeks.

Erica's House

I stayed with Erica for the next two weeks. Pearson and Perry joined me for the first week, as we helped wherever possible to prepare for Jim's funeral. Erica's house was soothing, spending time under the soaring ceilings in front of the stone fireplace gave us the space to register the tragedy. We began each morning in Erica's large, comfortable eat-in kitchen, which Erica had designed with cozy dinner-parties in mind. A famous designer had tried to come in, free of charge, to decorate the 1950's ranch-style home with big splashes of purple and gold, but Erica knew what she wanted. She had loved the kitschy feel of the original era. She purposefully sought out a 1950's atomic ranch home, reminiscent of the homes from her favorite old movies.

When we were kids she had always loved the dad's house in The Parent Trap and the cozy homes from TV shows like Leave it to Beaver and Donna Reid. She had laughed when she told me her friends and colleagues thought she was crazy, decorating her own house. But it made her happy, scouring the internet and antique stores for silly tins and splashy signs while everyone else had fancy decorators painting everything white and looking for gold and fuchsia artwork. My mom had laughed good-naturedly at her old-fashioned stone fireplace and wood floors, the whimsical prints on the walls. But Erica's home had a cozy feel that drew others to it, their stark and beautiful and frequently photographed homes sat empty as they convened on her comfortable and cheerful home, presided over by Angie.

I always enjoyed visiting my sister, I loved the basic simplicity and clean lines of the home, the view of the hills and flowers out the large picture windows, and the natural beauty of the wood floors and angled ceilings. Keeping true to the era, Erica had used muted tones of pink and baby blue set to a backdrop of rich wood and stone. Her home was comfortable first and foremost. The kitchen dominated by a large stone fireplace and a big farm table, a sliding door leading out to the vegetable and herb garden and splashing pond covered by a pergola. Truly her home was a sanctuary.

But the first morning it didn't feel like a sanctuary, we all kept remembering Jimmy. Erica dissolved into tears as she tried to eat a piece of toast, hiccuping that Jim had helped her install the pond, that Jim and Kelly had come over for dinner often sharing stories from the latest concert. I started crying too as I thought of Jim, a needle in his arm in the bathroom stall at The Fountain. I shook my head and tried to think of something else.

We got through our first few days, staying busy, helping Kelly as much as possible to arrange for the funeral. Nothing seemed real. My boys helped, mainly by being so alive and loving. Now that they were both older Pearson and Perry had a sweetness that I hadn't anticipated. Their support for Erica during this time made me proud. Perry, at 8, was generous and helpful, bringing both of us tea and trying to get his aunt to eat. 10-year-old Pearson, who shared his aunt's talent for the guitar, encouraged Erica to play her guitar too, to be distracted.

Nothing really helped, but I knew having us around helped her. I knew she felt responsible, like she could have stopped Jim. I felt responsible too, especially because of Ricky - why did

we let him in? No one said anything about Ricky in front of
Pearson or Perry, but we all were aware of his role in Jim's
death. I wondered if he would turn himself in. Or if someone
else would. I couldn't bear the thought of my sons having their
dad go to jail, but he had a responsibility for this mess. The
whole thing made me feel sick.

Erica was also concerned about Malcolm, though at this
point I don't even know if he could be considered her boyfriend.
I was less and less impressed with the guy the more I learned
about him. He was obviously not a prize, no matter how
amazing she told me he was. He hadn't been at her concert and
he hadn't even come to see her after Jim died. He was clearly
only concerned with his own life and Erica's concern about him
just made all of her grief about Jim worse.

Malcolm

Malcolm Jamison Smithe was powerful and wealthy, a successful music producer who had been stringing Erica along for three years. Forty years old, never married, Malcolm was considered one of the most eligible bachelors in town. With his thick black hair elegantly changing to silver and tall, muscular frame, Malcolm was handsome in that traditional way most women didn't question. His wealth and power made him even more sought after, though women didn't want to compete with Erica. Malcolm and Erica were often photographed together, he was the perfect candidate to accompany her on her various events and photo ops. Both knew the other gave them power and clout, but neither had ever been able to figure out how to have an actual relationship out of the spotlight.

Erica knew being a famous singer in a very popular band made her too cool to be wanting a baby, but she confided in me that she was experiencing pangs of longing every time she saw the latest baby bump or celebrity mom pushing a Bob stroller in a photo shoot. She had just turned twenty-eight and her rock star status didn't make her any less human than any other woman. At her last gynecological appointment Dr. Thursgood had asked if she had plans to get pregnant anytime soon, like it was a normal idea. At the appointment she had laughed like it hadn't mattered, but his words hit her like ice in the face. Really? Already?   She had considered getting married a couple of times. She thought of Carlos a fellow musician who she had dated a few years before. He would have been perfect, career-wise, but he hadn't been right for her. And now Malcolm, who hinted at that stability and long-term love but just didn't seem capable of seeing what marriage and a family could offer. In fact, Malcolm, couldn't even commit to dinner next week.

"I just want light and life in my house." Malcolm had cooed on their first date as they held hands walking through the rain. Erica had called me right after their date, she thought she had hit the jackpot - finally! - until she hadn't heard from him again for over two weeks, and then it was as if he had never said anything romantic.

When he had finally called her, way back three years ago, he had just chatted about his day, asked about her music, and hadn't mentioned their date at all. It was all she could do to not aggressively pursue him - she was Erica Princeton! But she had to have some pride - she somehow managed to stay busy with her band and her friends and hadn't broken down and called him. She and I had a pact that any time she felt compelled to call or text him she had to call or text me first. It kept her distracted, but she told me now she found herself bursting, wanting to ask him if he loved her, if he wanted to be with her forever, even if he just wanted to join her for dinner. But it didn't matter, nothing had ever quite come close to that first date.

I had given up wanting to hear about the Erica and Malcolm drama, though at first I had followed every detail. They started out so lovingly, three years earlier. Both were recently single and mutual friends had suggested to Erica that she call him. She had felt just brave enough and eager enough to get into the dating scene again that she had. Because of her level of fame and wealth she had discovered that men could be intimidated by her, so when he had suggested dinner during their first friendly phone call she was relieved. Maybe here was a man who would see her as a woman and not just a ticket to fame and fortune.

Their first date Malcolm had arrived at her front door after being cleared to go through her entry gate. He had given her a small but lovely bouquet of flowers when she opened the door, gazing subtly at her well-fitting jeans and silk shirt as he held out his arm for her. He held the door to his BMW as she climbed in, closing it considerately behind her. He smiled down at her as he pulled out, his kind, handsome face crinkling up as he joked that he hadn't been able to find her enormous house.

"Feel free to adjust the music, the heat, whatever." He said as he pulled out. She had laughed happily, she knew she liked this guy. His car was very clean but still lived-in, as if he had made a special effort but was still a normal person and not too uptight. He was very interested in her, listening closely as she shared about her family and band and interests.

"Do you ever miss Walla Walla?" He had asked after finding out her family still lived in her hometown.

"Oh yes, but I don't know how I could ever live there full time. My parents have pretty much retired and my sister has a family and they are really happy to just live a quiet life there. Sure, they come down to L.A. during the gray winters, but mainly they are just happy to take their dogs on walks and join their friends for dinner. I can see how they might love that lifestyle, it must be nice to just be relaxed and secure and not worry about what people are thinking or what you need to achieve."

"But you have this town in the palm of your hand!" He had declared, crinkling his brown eyes at her and leaning forward. "Don't you realize if you left what a big gap you would leave?"

She had laughed at his flattery, full of a warm glow from his attention and obvious attraction.

The rest of their evening had flown by. She told me she had barely been able to eat anything, though when she had first arrived and ordered a dark beer he had put his hand over his heart and looked at her like she was a recently discovered buried treasure.

"I think I'm in love!" He said cheerfully. "You drink dark beer? Most women just sip at a white wine and pick at a salad. You are a girl after my own heart."

Erica had giggled, his attention was like a warm blanket and she wanted more. When it was time to order she hadn't even had to muster any willpower to stay on her diet, she had been so smitten by his attention and sweetness that she had barely wanted to pick at her small green salad. Malcolm had seemed equally in tune with her, barely eating his steak. By the time the waitress had asked if they want dessert, Erica knew she would kiss him, already looking at his full mouth as he told her about his latest musicians.

Dinner had led to a walk where they had talked so much the evening had just slipped away. When she shivered, he slid off his large tweed jacket and, staring deeply in her eyes, he carefully covered her bare shoulders. The rain had been pelting all around them but she hadn't even noticed. When they arrived at a large puddle preventing them from crossing the street he had stopped, held out his hand, and told her to climb on up. She had laughed as he carried her on his back across the street, smelling his clean hair and feeling how warm he was through his cotton shirt. After a few blocks through the rain they came to a foot bridge over a small stream. She was full of optimism and energy, dashing up the three steps and to the middle of the bridge. She stopped, looking out over the small creek below. She sighed happily, feeling raindrops hit her cheeks. He reached her on the bridge and stood quietly next to her for a few minutes.

"I've always loved the water," he said, staring straight ahead. He had stood close to her and she could feel his firm arm as she leaned slightly into him.

She murmured that she did too, though she didn't have a chance to say anything more because she realized he was looking intently at her. She turned toward him and saw his dark eyes gazing intently at her. He touched her chin gently and tilted her face toward his, leaning down to give her a tender kiss. She felt herself responding to him immediately, groaning slightly at the lovely smoothness of his lips. He kissed her more deeply before moving back slightly and looking fully at her. He smiled, his eyes crinkling down at her.

He stood silently for a moment then spoke again, deep feeling making his deep voice crack. "I've been so lonely for such a long time. My house is so quiet since June moved out last summer. It needs a woman's touch, it needs light and life."

When she told me this that night we had both squealed, what a sweet thing to say! Erica had been surprised at his frank revelation, saying her heart had swelled at his words. Was he saying she might be the woman to bring light to his home? Even though his words could be taken as being forward she felt no fear or apprehension. She agreed, her house was dark and lonely too. Without saying anything more she nodded and then put both her arms around him in a big hug. He held her tightly, swaying slightly.

He chuckled softly and whispered, "You are so tiny and delicate. It makes me want to protect you."

"Thanks," she breathed, "you can be my protector."

He then took her by the hand and led her back across the bridge and down the steps.

The whole walk home, including when he carried her back over the large puddle again, they had held hands and looked deeply at each other. She was so enraptured by him that she couldn't stop looking at him and said she felt slightly dizzy, unlike any other experience she had ever known.

She had an early call at the studio the next day and needed to be well rested, so they reluctantly returned to his car and then to her house. They never stopped holding hands, he stroked her fingers and wrists as he drove, making her nearly wild with just that simple touch. By the time he stopped in front of her sweeping front entry she was tempted to invite him inside despite her deep beliefs that there was no faster way to lose a potential love interest - at least that was what all her girlfriends seemed to ever experience. Erica had always maintained a good distance from dates as a matter of protection and had decided that it was the best option for her sanity. This guy was different, but she still had her standards for herself. His regard and respect for her seemed to increase even more when she stopped at the door, gave him a big hug and a small kiss, and said good-bye.

"So, no boyfriend?" He asked, looking concerned.

She laughed, "No! No one. You?"

He laughed too, "No, no boyfriend. Or girlfriend either."

They both just stood there staring at each other grinning for a moment until she finally groped behind herself for the door handle and pushed her way inside. Calling a wistful good-bye she closed the door, but not before catching one last longing look from Malcolm.

As soon as she closed the door she hugged herself joyfully. Love! She was in love! She had danced around her beautiful marble and stone entryway for a few minutes before floating up to call me, to tell me about the glory of meeting such a wonderful man.

Noncommittal

The next morning she had woken full of energy and, yes, light and life. She had sang and hummed and danced all the way to the studio. She told me the guys in the band had teased her as she drifted dreamily through that days recording session, asking who she was thinking about. When she told them she had met Malcolm Jamison Smithe they had hooted at her.

"Smithe Records? You have to be kidding! No one has ever been able to get that guy to settle down," Jimmy had said, concern creasing is brow. "Don't get to far over your head, he's been known to string girls along."

Erica hadn't even listened, she knew what they had shared the night before was magic. She knew he would call, he would invite her to see his house, which she would give that feminine touch he was longing for. Their families would love each other. Their musical connections would make them the next power couple in town. He would look so handsome standing next to her at the celebrity events. They could work a few more years then buy a large estate in Walla Walla and retire near the river, have two or three kids, a couple of dogs.....

Then...nothing. He hadn't called. He hadn't invited her to see his large home devoid of love. He hadn't even arranged for a second date. Erica was so eager to talk to him that first night that she had practically had to sit on her hands to stop from calling him. Every woman who had been in the dating market for longer than a couple of weeks knew a man wanted to pursue. So she had tried to stay busy and distracted in hopes that he would call. The first night he didn't call she was slightly disappointed but knew he was probably waiting the requisite three days. The second and third day she was still patient. She called me and I tried to distract her, but she was anxious. As the days turned into weeks she knew he hadn't been able to follow through. For whatever reason, she would never know, Malcolm had not been able to be the man he hinted he could be.

Fifteen days later he called again. By this time so much time had passed that Erica had nearly forgotten. Nearly, but not quite, and after so much time she felt more irritated with him than interested, so their phone call had been strained and cold. He had ended by inviting her to a dinner hosted by one of his colleagues at Smithe Records, a sound mixer known as a genius in the editing room. She hadn't wanted to sound overeager but she had still readily agreed and had looked forward to the event with anticipation.

Unfortunately, when he had come to pick her up for this second date, exactly three weeks after the first, he acted as though they had never even shared the intimate moment on the bridge. And for the next three years Malcolm had never shown this hint of love again, except for on the occasion when Erica would get mad and refuse to see him or start to date someone else. Then Malcolm would desperately pursue her, write her a sweet note or send a bouquet of flowers. It was as if there were a wall between them. I listened sympathetically when she described his coldness, but less sympathetically when she described how he seemed to want to be the only man in her life. I hated seeing her so enthusiastic about someone who wasn't treating her well.

After a few more dates where he coldly and politely took her out, visited with her, then dropped her off at home, she finally broached the subject.

"What happened Malcolm?" She asked after pushing herself to muster up the courage to confront the issue.

He cocked his head to the side, "What do you mean?"

She felt angry at him. Was she just imagining that he had given her the sweetest kiss she'd ever experiencing? "This. Us. What was that amazing kiss on the bridge? The need for light and life? Where did you go?"

He had stopped smiling and looked at the ground. They were standing outside a crowded club, waiting to get in. Though they were both rich and she was famous they had still arrived late enough after an elegant dinner nearby that they had to wait for space to clear before they could enter. Neither minded because the night was beautiful.

"I'm sorry," he whispered, "I just got scared. After June left me it was like my heart froze. I want to love, I want to be with you, but whenever I think of trusting you I don't feel anything."

"What do you mean? It just takes time, just let me in. You mean so much to me." She had stepped toward him, putting her hand on his shoulder and looking intently into his kind brown eyes, so full of pain it hurt her to see it.

He shook his head, "No, Erica, you deserve better. I can't love. There is just blackness where my heart should be. I can't trust. I can't love. I wouldn't be able to give you what you need."

Though she knew he spoke the truth, she continued to see him because she figured eventually his heart would thaw. Eventually he would realize he did love her, he could trust her. She felt so much love and such a certainly about him being right for her that she was sure someday he would be able to reciprocate. Hearing her rationale was maddening, I decided she must not really want to be with someone full time and just enjoyed having someone part-time.

He never did thaw. He was unreliable, calling so infrequently she would think he had given up on her entirely. Or calling to ask her to attend events with him at the last minute, dates she hated herself for agreeing to attend. The rest of us were so tired of hearing her confusion and dissatisfaction with the Malcolm situation we would just cut her off if she mentioned his name.

"Let him go," Angie sighed when she brought him up.

"He's never going to commit to you or anyone else," Angie's daughter, Samantha declared, rolling her eyes.

I tried to be a good sounding board, but I could only listen to her describe Malcolm's latest broken promise or disappearance for a few minutes before casually changing the subject.

Only our mother ever had anything positive to say. She was convinced that their perfect compatibility would certainly trump Malcolm's fear of commitment. She was his biggest champion, calling Erica regularly to get an update. If Erica ever complained about not hearing from him for too long or Malcolm not holding her hand in public or Malcolm being overly friendly with other women, Adelaide would chide her. She would instruct her to give him space, he would come around when the time was right.

But the time was never right. Malcolm continued to treat her kindly, to invite her on occasional sporadic dates, to give her flowers or a gift if she started to lose interest, stringing her along so successfully that before she knew it three years had passed.

She dated other men, whenever she had any opportunity - though her heart wasn't in it. And she was seen with Malcolm so often, photographed so frequently with him at public events, that most men didn't even bother to show interest because it was clear that she belonged to Malcolm. Even if he didn't care that she belonged to him. Even if he didn't belong to her. Even if he was just wasting her time.

Sometimes she would give up completely. She would even get mad at him. One evening, after they had been dating off and on for nearly two years, she had gotten upset on the drive home. She called me in tears afterwards to tell me all about it

"You won't even hold my hand when we walk in!" She had exclaimed abruptly as he drove smoothly through her hilly neighborhood.

They had just been to a record release party for a young soloist he was representing.

Malcolm had patted her knee playfully, "I'm sorry. You know how caught up I get when we go to those things. You know I forget everything but working the crowd."

Usually Erica would quietly nod and try to forget it, but this night she was feeling particularly upset. It was only a few weeks before her 27th birthday and she was starting to feel the pressure to marry and have babies. She had never told Malcolm her dream of becoming his wife, moving near her parents, raising babies, but she wished she could.

"I'm not ok with it Malcolm! I want more. You are not there for me when I need you. What do you want from me? I think you just want me so you can say you know me, so you can show me off. I don't think you care about me, as a person, at all! In fact, don't call me any more. I don't even want to know you."

They had pulled in front of her large house and she had opened the door and started to get out.

"Wait Erica!" He had said, clearly upset at her outburst. "You can't mean that. You are really special to me. Don't just end it."

Seeing that her words hurt him made her soften. She turned back toward him and looked up at him, touching his arm.

"Then let me know how you feel about me," she whispered.

He opened and closed his mouth a few times, but no words came out.

"I - I….can't. I just can't." His face, usually so confident and cheerful, was full of pain. She told me she felt a rush of love for him as she looked at him, understanding he truly did love her, though just couldn't trust in her or anyone else enough to declare it.

But she had to move on. She shook her head as she patted his cheek. "I wish you could Malcolm. Good-bye."

And she had managed to stay away from him for a month that time, I was so proud of her. Eventually, though, he was able to persuade her to see him again. That had been the time he called her drunk, in the middle of the night.

"Hello?" She had groggily picked up her cell phone without even looking at the Caller ID.

"I love you Erica. You know I love you." It was Malcolm. She told me she could hear him slurring his words together, she could practically feel him swaying as he hollered into his phone. It was the first time he had ever declared his love for her.

She said she felt a confusing mix of sadness and frustration and giddy joy at his proclamation, though her common sense prevailed as she realized he was declaring his love drunk while they were broken up. Would they ever have a heathy relationship? We all wondered why she put up with the hot and cold, but she just couldn't seem to break free completely.

Currently they were in that uncomfortable place of dating where Malcolm was beginning to take Erica for granted and Erica was beginning to resent his lack of interest or commitment. Right before the concert she told me she figured she would probably break it off with him for good soon, she was tired of the roller coaster. She just wished she could be with someone she got along with, like Malcolm, but who was also steady. She had chuckled, Malcolm had said that same thing to her the last time they had broken up and he had begged her to get back.

Destined for...Loneliness?

At the urging of all of us who were absolutely fed up with her continued saga of Malcolm and his lack of commitment, Erica would agree to dating other men on occasion. She knew since Malcolm wasn't ready to commit her best option would be to stay busy and date whenever it worked out. The guys in the band always had friends that were interested in taking her out, but she was very wary. So many men seemed only interested in her wealth or status, in what she could do for them.

She and I both agreed: after awhile going on dates can begin to feel like just a series of job interviews. What do you do? What do you do for fun? Did you grow up here? Are you close to your family? What do you hope to do in the future? It was exhausting. I sympathized with her, I'd been single for years too. I never had very much to say after the preliminary questions were out of the way, and it just didn't end up being that much fun. Erica was looking for someone would just make her laugh or be able to play music...or just like her for her. Not because she was Erica Princeton, lead singer for The Flying Foes.

Two weeks before, she had called me to tell me about a young man she had gone out with, she had been set up by her hair stylist. He was younger than her, only twenty-five, but this was not a problem because she was so youthful and attractive she was used to younger men being interested. He was an investment banker who had appeared on a late-night talk show and her stylist had done his hair (thick and black Erica, you'll love him!).

But Erica hadn't loved him. Oh, sure, for about three days she thought maybe he had potential. His obvious wealth and success made them equals in the status department, making it so she wasn't quite as suspicious about what he might want from her. And he had been an exuberant texter, carrying on a steady stream of friendly banter for the three days before they met. She enjoyed a fun text-message volley on occasion, if she had time. Though she did wonder how he had time to send so many texts if he was supposedly such a busy executive. It was fun, though, to get texts like:

<What are you doing, Rock Star?>

<Just waiting to meet with the band to go over our new set.>

<Sounds fascinating. Are you as cute in person as in the magazines?>

His flirtation had continued on steadily for three days, and she had to admit she was looking forward to meeting someone so clearly confident. But when they had finally met up, at the new Roof Top restaurant, she had initially been quite interested. As her stylist had promised, his hair was thick and black and perfectly accented his chiseled jaw and deep blue eyes. He looked like Christopher Reeves in the original Superman. His manners had been impeccable too, pulling the chair out for her, asking the sommelier to let her sip the wine before serving it, listening attentively as she briefly described her day.

But after two glasses of wine he was a little looser and had started talking about his childhood in San Diego. He scowled when he told her his mother had stayed home to care for him while his dad earned a huge amount of money as the CEO of an engineering company. He said his dad had been very harsh, hitting him and his younger brother on occasion.

As soon as Erica told me this, I got suspicious.

"His dad hit him when he was little?" I asked.

"Yes, but it got worse." She told me she started paying close attention as he calmly revealed his experience. She leaned forward a little and looked carefully at his handsome face.

"Did your dad ever hit your mom?" She asked, trying not to sound too anxious.

He shrugged, scooting back and propping his foot on his knee. "Sure, sometimes. But only when she deserved it."

Erica couldn't help herself, "What! No one ever deserves to be hit! How could your mom - or you - possibly deserve to be hit?"

Realizing he had said something offensive, he held his hands up, "Hey, hey, no big deal! She's fine, she knows how to stay in line. Sheesh, what's the problem?" His handsome face didn't cover his scorn as he defended his dad's right to beat his family.

Erica didn't take the issue any further, this man clearly didn't see anything wrong with physical abuse and punishment. She was anxious to get away from him, suddenly aware that this man, no matter how successful, well-mannered, and attractive, would never be someone she would want to spend time with again.

He seemed to sense the shift in her attitude, though we both wondered if he had enough awareness to know why. They wrapped up their date soon after and she left quickly, very glad to be escaping unscathed.

Once home after yet another failed date, Erica changed into her favorite cashmere pants and cardigan before calling me to commiserate.

"Better alone than poorly accompanied," I told her in consolation.

"Yeah, but being well accompanied sure would be nice."
She sighed, "If only Malcolm would come around...or if I
could just meet someone kind. Funny. Real. Oh well."

Erica had one real boyfriend, once. Carlos Jennings. We all
thought she would marry him. He had been a singer too, one of
the backup singers on another show that filmed at the same time
as Kids Rock, Fanfare, and he had understood her in ways that
other guys never had. They had met just after she had returned
with the band to Los Angeles, just as The Flying Foes were
starting to get really famous. Carlos had a beautiful voice, deep
and smooth, and he loved to harmonize. He sang commercials
and had performed in three off-broadway performances in New
York before returning to Los Angeles where he felt there were
more opportunities. When Erica met him they had both waiting
in the Green Room before going live on the Josh Carlsson Live!
Show. They were with a large group of their cast mates from
their years as child stars for a reunion show and they had hit it
off right away.

The first few months had been great. For the first time Erica
was in a relationship that was comfortable and easy, not calling
me wondering if he actually liked her or if he was just using her
for her fame. But eventually he had started getting too clingy,
wanting to spend every moment with her, tagging along
whenever she went out with her friends, even wanting to join her
at the gym and shopping. He hadn't meant any harm, but she
had eventually grown tired of having him around so often.
When she finally got up the nerve to tell him how she felt he had
not wanted to let it end, though he did go away after awhile. To
this day, if she ever gets too down about Malcolm not spending
enough time with her, I can always jokingly remind her that
Carlos might be available.

And now a week after Jim's death Malcolm still had not come around. She seemed to think his presence would help her deal with Jim's loss, like he could give her strength. It was frustrating to watch her check her cell phone and then see her disappointment when there was no text message. But maybe it gave her something to distract her from the tragedy of Jim's death.

The Funeral

"Move on already, it's been a week. So you lost a druggie band member, it happens. Pick yourself up by the bootstraps and get back out there." Malcolm said.

He was adjusting his tie in her front mirror, looking at himself as he spoke. He had come over to accompany Erica to the funeral, the first time I'd seen him since I'd arrived. He had called before 8:00 that morning, the first time he'd called in over a week. Erica had woken early to go jogging and I was up to see Pearson and Perry off. Our parents were taking my boys home and they had left early that morning. We were enjoying our coffee when she heard the buzzing of her phone and saw it was Malcolm.

"Hi Mal, thanks for calling." She said eagerly, I rolled my eyes at Angie who was preparing breakfast at the stove.

"You are not still in bed are you?" I could hear his loud voice booming over the cell phone. Malcolm didn't usually exchange pleasantries, he claimed to be too busy for them.

"No, I'm up. I have a lot to do today, it is Jim's funeral."

"Yeah, about that, I know how you need me to go with you and all, but I have an important meeting at 3:00, so we better take separate cars. You understand."

Malcolm had arrived a few minutes late but didn't seem to concerned about arriving on time to the funeral. I could tell Erica was getting fed up with him, she didn't even acknowledge him as we walked out the door.

So many people were in attendance at Jim's funeral that we had to have Angie drop us off before looking for a parking spot further away. Almost every seat was already filled, but Erica and I moved to the front of the cathedral to sit with Ben and Carlisle behind Jim's parents and sister. I was glad she didn't try to look for Malcolm or save him a seat; maybe this would be the wake up call Erica finally needed about Malcolm. Especially when, right in the middle of Ben's eulogy, a cell phone deedle-deedled from the back.

Turning my head slightly, I was able to see Malcolm jumping up and pressing buttons, hurrying out the door. As the large doors closed behind him I heard him answer the phone call. What a jerk. When we emerged from the funeral thirty minutes later he was still hollering into the phone. He barely looked at her tear-streaked face before jumping into his illegally-parked BMW and speeding off. Most people were much too concerned about Jim and his family to even notice Malcolm's terrible behavior, but Erica had noticed, and I could tell by the determined set to her mouth that she was fed up.

Attempting to Heal

Erica and I returned from the funeral drained, but she planned to spend the rest of the day working on music for an upcoming studio session. She had written three songs with Jim just weeks before his death and she knew their fans would go crazy over his last work. But without at least five more songs to go along with them the band wouldn't have enough to record an entire album, leaving all of Jim's hard work lost. She had to write and it had to reflect the spirit of her best friend. How was she going to do this?

Entering her spacious, shade dappled sun room she used for her studio, Erica picked up her acoustic Fender guitar and began to strum the punk baseline Ben had prepared for their opening song. After a few minutes she leaned back and sighed.

"Oh Penny, I'm trying to clear my mind so I can make room for the lyrics, they're sure to come. But I keep seeing Jim's body."

Shaking her head, she kept at it, looking up at the trees visible out the large picture windows of the sunroom on occasion. But the lyrics were all simple repetitive pleas for help.

Jim Jim Jim

You never let us in in in
You followed after sin sin sin

Erica sighed, I looked up from the book I was trying to read.

"Writing at this point is futile." She told me, "Right now I need friendship and distraction, not a crunched time schedule. These lyrics are stupid and trite."

Jotting down the lyrics, silly though they were, she then got up and opened the French door to the brick patio. The hanging bougainvillea and ferns tumbling over the stucco walls. The wrought iron cafe table and chairs and the singing of birds were beautiful, though she still sighed in agitation.

I joined her on her stone patio as the sun began to set.

"This can usually bring the inspiration if I need to begin a new song, but tonight no lyrics float to my head beyond 'I'm sorry.' Over and over, repeating miserably through my head." She said softly. "I'm sorry Jim. I'm sorry I couldn't be there for you. I'm sorry I didn't stop you from going with the Rhodes, I'm sorry I didn't stick closer to you when we got so famous and you didn't know how to handle it. I'm sorry Jim." She dissolved into tears. "I can't think of anything worth writing. All my lyrics are sad and not at all appropriate for ska or punk, more like depressing ballads."

I hated seeing my little sister like this, I didn't know what to do. I made the only suggestion I could think of, "Do you want to see if Samantha is around? Maybe we could go out somewhere? A little change of scenery?" Erica always got more and more melancholy if she was in a quiet environment with too few people around her, I hoped something a little more lively would help her.

She nodded, "Good idea."

Picking up her cell phone, she texted Samantha Thankfully Samantha was available and said she could be at Erica's house in thirty minutes, Erica seemed slightly less distraught at the idea of The Canyon Club, the ultra-exclusive bar/cafe where she could be guaranteed to be left alone by photographers. Since Samantha's mom, Angie, was Erica's assistant and lived in the guest apartment, Samantha already spent a lot of time at Erica's pretty house. But she had recently purchased a condo in nearby Beachwood Canyon where she and her husband, a sound technician, were happily enjoying their life.

Throwing a soft black cashmere cardigan over her skinny jeans and cotton tank top, Erica added a little lip gloss and blush before brushing her long hair. When Samantha arrived a few minutes later she was calm and looking forward to going out for a couple of hours. As we drove through the winding tree-lined streets toward The Canyon Club Samantha and I listened to Erica lament the loss of Jim.

"Why? Why would he have relapsed? Everything was going so well for him, for all of us." Erica was saying.

Samantha shook her head, "I have no idea. I wish we could just go back in time, just tell those stupid Rhodes to go away."

Erica took a deep breath and straightened her back with resolve. "I have to distract myself. Malcolm thinks I can get back to work and record the album anyway, even without Jim. I couldn't even write one verse, forget about an entire song much less an album. I have to get out, think about something else for a little bit. I hope someone good is playing tonight, it's always inspiring to hear good music."

Not All Fans Are Nice

When we pulled in front of the cheerfully cozy club Samantha handed her keys to the valet before walking into the brick and wood entryway. As usually happened whenever Erica went into a public place, the friendly buzz of the crowd diminished markedly as they walked in. Erica was a professional and very used to the effect she had on a room, though she pretended not to notice as she smiled and waved to an acquaintance seated across the room. Sweeping across the intimate club to the best booth located at the back near the fireplace, Erica held her head high and slid into across the black leather seat. She had barely had time to shrug off her cardigan when a young couple approached the table.

"Erica Princeton? I can't believe you are here." The man said. He was very thin. Dark-framed glasses and slicked back hair marked him as trendy and in the know. He wore an expression of disdain as he leaned in toward her.

"How dare you show your face after what you let happen to Jim Jackson." He hissed, his voice and face full of rage, "druggies like you don't deserve to just walk free after destroying someone as special as him!"

The girl with him, equally thin and cool with dreadlocks tucked under a large red knit cap, glared at Erica with hatred.

"Yeah, you have some nerve showing your face out here so soon after his tragedy. Jim Jackson didn't deserve to die! It's musicians like you and your loser band that give all of us musicians a bad name. Shame on you Erica Princeton!'

And with that evil pronouncement the two turned abruptly and huffed off, full of indignation, and with a complete misunderstanding of the situation.

Samantha pushed herself up from the table and followed after them with a quick look of sympathy at Erica who was trying to swallow the tears that were springing to her eyes.

Tapping the young man on his shoulder as he started to sit a few feet away at the bar, she thrust her face right up into his.

"Who do you think you are, pendejo?" Samantha spat at him, "How dare you accuse Erica of having anything to do with Jim's death? You have no idea what the situation is, just because some idiotic tabloid claims Erica uses too gives you no right to go around accusing her of anything. You, sir, are a useless POS. And you, ma'am, are equally misinformed. I hope you both rot!"

Spinning on her heel, Samantha flounced back to Erica to console her. The couple stared at her, flabbergasted at her vitriolic speech. I noticed the bartender whispering to them as she sat down across from Erica.

"Are you OK?" Samantha asked, all traces of anger replaced with a caring tone.

Erica nodded, her eyes still moist but her eye makeup intact. She did not often have negative run-ins with the public, but growing up with two famous parents had given her enough experience that she knew how to handle it by staying calm and pretending it didn't bother her. But this was not just a conservative mother insulted by her lyrics or harsh rock and roll life, this was a personal attack blaming her for Jim's death. She was pale and clearly shaken by the experience.

Had it ended here Erica might have been able to play it off and maybe even been able to enjoy a beer and listen to the soft jazz band just beginning on stage. But just then the bartender who had been whispering to the accusatory couple appeared at their table.

"I'm sorry Miss Princeton," he said, unable to meet her gaze, "but we have this table reserved for another guest. You'll have to wait in the lobby for another table to open up." His eyes darted guiltily around the room, landing everywhere but on Erica or Samantha or me.

Samantha once again started to defend Erica, she drew herself up to her full five-foot-three-inches and said loudly, "Excuse me? We will stay here as long as we want!"

Erica reached across the table to her friend and shook her head, "No Sam, if they want to treat me like this they can. I can take my business elsewhere." And with her head held high, she stood up and made a dignified exit.

Samantha, unable to take the mistreatment silently, glared at the bartender, now back to whispering to the cool couple, and spat out, "We won't forget this!"

On the street, we waited for the valet to bring Samantha's black Bently. The ride home was quiet, we had all lost any desire to be out, and the evening traffic was frustratingly busy. By the time we pulled back through the gate Erica's tears were falling freely.

"I'm sorry Samantha," she said quietly as we got out, "I guess I should just be alone for awhile. I think I need a break."

Samantha gave her a sympathetic smile before pulling away, she knew Erica was right. Before going very far she pulled out her phone and dictated a quick text to her mom asking her to check up on Erica.

Loyal and loving as always, Angie quickly left her pretty cottage to join Erica and me in the sun room overlooking the patio dappled with little tea lights. She listened quietly as Erica talked about Jim, about her experience at the club, about her inability to write, about Malcolm and his coldness. Erica cried a little, but by the time she was done talking she felt a little better.

"What should I do Angie? I just need to get away. I need a change of scenery, being here alone or being harassed by people out there doesn't help me. I need to do something else."

Angie smiled gently at the younger woman, "Maybe it is time to go home? Your parents and Penny have wanted you to go up for a visit. Take a break. Go home. Clear your head in that little town. I will go with you, we will make life better with a new outlook."

Erica smiled weakly, "I think you may be right. I do need to go home. Let me call my mom."

As she slipped out to the back patio with her phone, I nodded at Angie. Once again she had the right solution. Of course Erica should come home.

Childhood Home

One week later Erica, Angie, and I were stepping off the small airplane onto the black landing strip at the tiny Walla Walla airport. Carrying her little suitcase, her hair tucked into a baseball cap, eyes hidden behind large mirrored aviator sunglasses, Erica was as incognito as she could manage. No one looked at her twice as she walked through the sliding door through the small crowd waiting for family. Our mother, Adelaide Princeton was already there waiting with Pearson and Perry. She had made no attempt to disguise herself, her white-blonde hair piled on top of her head, a silky purple pantsuit trimmed with silver sequins and a fur stole completed the look. Despite her obvious movie star status, however, the good people of Walla Walla left her alone. Most were so caught up with greeting their own families they didn't even look at her. The few who did notice her and, subsequently, Erica, politely gave them space and privacy.

"Erica! Pen! Angie! I'm over here!" She called, waving a flowered handkerchief over her head, though there was no way we could miss her in the small lobby.

I smiled despite myself. Our mother may have been over the top, a rose amongst buttercups, but her obvious love and excitement at seeing us was the balm Erica needed after her past difficult two weeks.

I gave my sons big hugs before we started walking to the car. They talked over each other telling me all about their week at home without me.

"Is this all you have?" Addie asked, her brow nearly furrowing through her regular dose of Botox treatment. Erica had a small suitcase and an even smaller purse over her shoulder.

Erica shook her head and walked with her mom, Angie, and me toward the small but full parking lot. Only our mother would think more than one suitcase was necessary for a trip to Walla Walla. As they got settled into her mother's perfectly cared for Gran Marquis sedan, Adelaide gushed on about her latest home remodeling project. Adelaide and Bruce Princeton owned one of the finer homes in Walla Walla, a stately mansion on Palouse, the winding tree-lined street near the center of town. Complete with an indoor pool, large glass sunroom, third story studio and walled garden, the mansion was nearly perfect when they had first purchased it many years before. Their busy schedule had prevented them from spending much time there, though, and it hadn't had much done to it for years. Now, however, Adelaide had time to engage in one of her favorite activities: decorating. The kitchen had not been redone since the early 1970's and had the gold and brown accents to prove it. Adelaide had gone through the proper channels to get the historical home updated to a pleasant mixture of period-appropriate with modern amenities. She was currently working with an architect and a contractor to create a kitchen and dining area worthy of the finest magazine spread - a likely possibility considering her track record for fixing up older homes.

"But this is it!" Adelaide was gushing on, "we are not going to live anywhere else now. No more traveling, no more buying new houses in every new filming location. Your dad is so happy to be home again, to be away from the rat race. He loves it here and wouldn't dream of leaving. So now my job is to make our home my crowning glory, the culmination of all my years of decorating homes."

I watched Erica lean back in the passenger seat, enjoying the ride and listening to our mom's happy chatter. Being away from the bustle of Hollywood was already settling over her. Maybe we could pick up a good daily yoga class while she was here, walk every morning, read some good books. She could play her guitar, listen to music in one of the little places downtown…and then I remembered Jimmy, how much he and Erica had enjoyed downtown Walla Walla, the music and nightlife. I watched her sigh. We were all sad, but maybe being back here would help her to just feel her grief and heal through it.

As we pulled into the circular driveway, Erica looked at the Tudor home where we had spent our happy elementary school years. Our parents had always maintained it as their primary residence, though all of us had spent a lot of time in Los Angeles when her career had begun to heat up. But in the intervening years she hadn't gotten to spend nearly enough time in the spacious though cozy home. Blonde beechwood floors, high ceilings, crystal chandeliers, and little window-seat reading nooks had made the home a sanctuary even before she had become so recognizable that going in public became an ordeal. Her own childhood bedroom was still decorated beautifully: a large white canopy bed, blue Oriental rugs, a large fireplace, and a window seat overlooking the centurion trees in the back yard. Erica pulled her bag out of the car and told us she planned to spend some time alone in front of the fireplace.

When we had moved to Walla Walla Erica had attended school at nearby Sharpstein Elementary, Erica's only opportunity to ever attend a public school. Though large by Walla Walla standards, 600 students was small compared to any of the L.A.

Schools we had attended before or since. The 100 year old school building held many happy memories for both of us, but for Erica the friendships she forged had long been neglected in her whirlwind of fame. Erica asked if any of her friends from that time were still around and if they would still remember her as the silly, bookish girl she had been before she became a screaming punk band singer.

I assured her that whenever I saw any of them around town they always asked after her - and not about her rock star career, either, but just about her.

She still talked with Geri Wellsley and Amanda Jones a few times a year, but I knew she would want to see them to catch up in person. Then she asked about Charlie Jones, her first crush.

"Do you ever see him?" She asked me, "He was so sweet in elementary school. Do you think he will remember me? I never talk to Amanda about him, it's just too awkward." We laughed when we remembered how she had followed him around, much like me with Raymond.

"Yes, he's still around," I told her, "in fact I saw him just before I came out to L.A. Didn't mom mention to you? He's her contractor for the latest project."

The look on her face let me know she was carrying around a lot more feeling for Charlie than she had ever let on. She told me about the last time she had seen him, back when she had lived in Portland and had shared a loft with Charlie's sister Amanda.

"He was always so kind, Pen, and I was just so nervous about him! I couldn't really be myself. I would act cool, bounce around all over the place. I wish I could go back in time, just be honest with him and tell him how I felt."

I understood, I didn't mention Raymond. I was still embarrassed about my interest in him all those years ago.

"Well," I told her, "Amanda told us at the last book club that he had gotten divorced. I guess his wife hadn't wanted kids and he did…so she left him and moved to Seattle. She's going to art school."

She looked so hopeful I was surprised, I hadn't realized my sister still liked Charlie so much.

Many of our cousins still lived in town, though our mom gave her a hard time about how infrequently she called or visited with them. But I knew they understood and every time we got together it was as if no time had passed. I had already contacted everybody and we had a couple of fun nights planned. We didn't want to trap her into a time commitment during her visit, but seeing her face relax for the first time in two weeks I wondered if maybe she might want to stay longer than the four days she had planned. I hoped Ben and Carlisle would understand, without Jimmy they were all drifting.

Her Rise to Fame

Erica hadn't intended to be famous, but with a famous
writer/producer father and movie star mother it had come easily
for her. When she was in the sixth grade she was a cheerful girl
full of love for any popular boy band. She had a small group of
friends including Geri and Amanda all eager to grow up who all
wore too much sparkly makeup. At that point in her life she had
a passion for making chocolate chip cookies, a fascination with
architectural drawings, and a desire to be a brain surgeon.
Although our dad was busy, we both had our own lives and we
barely noticed his work projects. We had lived with our parents
in a gated community in Hollywood as younger girls, but we
barely remembered it. So when we sat down for dinner one
evening with another older couple, long-time friends of our
parents, we hadn't thought much about them being there beyond
saying hello and making polite conversation.

Our parents' friends, Russell and Edith Silverman had
known Bruce and Adelaide since they had first moved to Los
Angeles twenty-five years before. The two couples had both
been successful in the film and music industries, collaborating on
various projects and celebrating each other as they climbed to
astronomical heights of success. The Silvermans had never had
children and had taken a special interest in both Erica and me.

Of course with me, they had enjoyed seeing my latest art project or hearing about what I was reading, but with Erica they had often listened to her sing or recite a poem or watched her dance. But this evening they seemed particularly interested in Erica.

"So Erica," Mr. Silverman asked her, squinting down at her with particular attention, "how is school going? What are you most interested in? Do you still sing in the choir?"

"Oh yes!" Erica had declared, "Choir is my favorite. We are singing songs from Oliver right now, I wish I could play Nancy some day. I love that song she sings with Oliver."

"Are you interested in acting? I know you always were as a younger girl," Mr. Silverman continued.

Erica continued on happily, "Sure! We don't have a theater or drama class yet, but in high school I might get to be in a play. My mom let me do the Children't Theater last summer too. I got to play a knight!"

Erica didn't notice Mr. Silverman making eye contact with our dad over the dinner table. Bruce Princeton was shaking his head but smiling, pushing his hands down as if to tell his friend to slow down.

But Mr. Silverman did not slow down, he had a plan.

"What would you think of auditioning for a TV show now?" He asked her.

Erica stopped talking mid-sentence. She had been regaling them with a story about a boy in her choir class, Charlie, and how talented a singer he was. But when Mr. Silverman asked about an audition she turned fully toward him.

"An audition? I love auditions! What is it for? Is it TV? My mom retired, she wouldn't do TV anyway, she says it's tacky. Ooops." She slapped her own hand over her mouth, realizing she was talking to a man whose career was based on TV.

But Mr. Silverman wasn't at all insulted. He laughed. "No, I understand, not all TV is worth watching. But my company and I write and create and produce high-quality shows that people will want to watch. We have one in the works right now that you might just be interested in, it's called 'Kids Rock."

Erica looked between her parents, me, and Mr. and Mrs. Silverman, were they joking? She hoped not, she was beginning to like the sound of this.

A few months later she had joined Jim and the rest of the Kids Rock cast and started on her path of fame. Now that we were back in Walla Walla we were both reminded of Jimmy when he was younger, when he would come to visit with Erica. I hoped this would help her reach some closure and work through her pain.

Be Assertive

At age thirteen, when she had just begun working on Kids Rock, Erica had struggled initially. Roxana Shilling, the beautiful young actress who played Erica's best friend on the show, had decided to make destroying Erica her hobby. Though she played friendly, cheerful Sarah Graham on the show, in real life Roxana could be sharp-tongued and unkind. She would pretend to be friendly but could turn mean in an instant. She enjoyed complaining about anything she could pick apart. And there was no one she loved to pick apart more than Erica. Though both girls were raised in Hollywood families, our parents had made it a priority to give us the most normal life possible. Unlike Roxana, who had been filming commercials since age three, our parents had kept both of us focused on school, friendships, sports, and family activities until Erica finally begged them to let her audition for the program.

Roxana seemed angry and jealous - was it that they both came from wealthy families, so Roxana was not special compared to Erica? Was it that Roxana's parents treated her like a commodity? Or was it just that they were working so closely together and Roxana enjoyed looking for the worst in all situations? Our mom was convinced it was because Roxana, though a good enough gymnast and dancer, lacked musical talent. Whatever it was, Erica and I had long ago given up wondering about Roxana's motivations, especially after how she had turned out. But at the time, when Roxana would spread unkind rumors to the other kids on the cast, or, in a falsely kind tone, criticize every small move Erica made, or purposefully exclude Erica at every opportunity, Erica felt her world was ending. At first she called me almost nightly to describe Roxana's treatment, I had felt so helpless, wishing I could be there to defend her.

This is where Erica first met Angelica, just a couple of months into the show. Erica was hiding in the costume room, sobbing after Roxana had organized an outing to the water slide park for all the young cast members - all the young cast members except Erica. Oh, she had invited Erica, she had just made sure it was when Erica would be filming a beach scene with the adults actors who played her parents.

Angie had consoled Erica plus she had intervened by talking to the director to arrange a different time for filming. Erica had been able to go to the water slide park, though Angie had never been able to make Roxana be polite.

From then on Angie had been Erica's advocate, and eventually Adelaide's too when our parents hired her as Erica's assistant. If Bruce wasn't available to defend them, Angie would. Or her oldest daughter Samantha, who was only a year older than Erica, but possessed her mother's strength and confidence. My mom and Erica were so dependent on Angie to defend them or help them get what they needed that they relied on her for even the smallest trouble - Angie yelled. Erica and Adelaide cried. Problem solved.

Unless Angie was not around.

And this is where Erica struggled. She couldn't defend herself in even the most mundane circumstances, but it wasn't usually a problem. Lately though she had been thinking she should try to learn to be a little more assertive. Just recently she had called me, upset. She had been at a yoga class at an upscale gym when a woman had taken her spot when she went to grab a strap and block. Erica knew the woman had done it on purpose, Erica had arrived early just to get the coveted front and center spot. But, being unable to defend herself and not being able to talk either Angie or Samantha into joining her at yoga, Erica had been forced to get a new mat and go to the back of the room. She seethed the first fifteen minutes of class, practicing mentally how she should have spoken up for herself.

I was more of a happy medium between Erica and Angie. After my years living with Ricky I went through a lot of counseling and I learned a lot of techniques for standing up for myself. I wish sometimes I could be more like Angie or Samantha, especially in situations like the one at the bar in Los Angeles. I wish I could have marched up to that horrible couple that insulted my sister, like Samantha had. But I've come to accept my gentle nature and am proud of my ability to firmly defend myself if necessary. Both Erica and I often wish we were better at defending ourselves though.

Girls Night

Erica's closest friends Geri Wellsley and Amanda Jones had lived in Walla Walla their entire lives. Whenever I got together with Erica and our friends I was always so grateful for the life our parents had given us here in a small town. My own closest friend from school, Christina Hill, had recently moved back from Seattle. She and I had been close to Geri all through school and Amanda was a good friend from our book club. But whenever Erica came home we all eagerly gathered together. Erica was the spark that made any gathering exciting, even on a night like tonight when she was clearly subdued.

After giving her their condolences, we moved on to other subjects. Christina had left a career in finance and come home to study in the viticulture program and was now an unabashed wine snob. She had arrived with three very expensive bottles of local wine. After the first bottle of L'Eclole Merlot our conversation got to be more from the heart.

We asked Amanda how everything was going for her in the dating world. Divorced for five years, the mother of three school-age children, Amanda had taught high school French for 7 years. She confided that her ex-husband still wasn't paying child support, so she was watching her house and car fall apart while working long hours at a thankless job. Seeing our faces, Amanda tried to lighten the mood.

"Not to worry! Will owes me eighty-thousand dollars! I'm sure some day when I really need it he'll come through for me." She smiled and we all ventured a light laugh.

But we thought of her ex-husband and it made us all mad. When Amanda had lived with Erica in Portland she and Carlisle had begun spending time together. They had been a really good match, we'd all been happy to see the serious Amanda lighten up around the even more serious Carlisle. Carlisle had loved to tease her, telling her fantastically fake stories that she always believed, then laughing when he revealed the truth. They'd been really cute.

Then this guy named Will had appeared out of nowhere from one of Amanda's classes. He'd been really persuasive and aggressive and the next thing anyone knew they'd gotten married. He'd turned out to be a big loser, though, unable to keep a job, rude, and unfaithful. They stayed married long enough to have three great kids, but now Amanda was on her own and Will was long gone.

Amanda told us she hated being a burden on her big brother, though she often traded meals for minor home repairs. I saw Erica perk up at this mention of Charlie. I could see her plotting a little, maybe thinking about what she would cook for him.

"What about your exciting life as a single woman, Amanda? How is it?" Christina asked. We all eagerly leaned forward. Though Amanda, Erica, and I were all single, Amanda was the only one who ever seemed to have any interesting dating stories.

She rolled her eyes. "Well, I've been taking a break from dating for the past six months. I was having fun at first, meeting different people. But the last two were total duds, they weren't worth my time. One was a successful doctor with his own private practice, but after three months he told me my kids and I were "not the whole package," he needed some trophy wife to tote around to doctor-type events.

"Jerk." Geri said.

"The second was a waiter at a fancy restaurant, this was last winter. We started out so with so much enthusiasm, mainly because he was much younger." She blushed. "He was five years younger than me. But I eventually came to my senses about him too. Maybe it's time to just give up on the whole thing."

Geri promised us she was happy, really happy. But then she confessed that if she stopped to think too long about anything she sometimes felt sad.

"So," she was telling us, her big blue eyes full of pain, "I just don't stop. I know I can't really complain, I know. Listen to me with my first world problems. But…I am just so embarrassed by my weight, by how fat I've gotten. You guys are so thin, I can't believe I'm confiding in you."

She looked at the counter, her pretty face full of such sadness I hurt for her. Geri had been beautiful and popular in high school, thin and blonde and a cheerleader. My opinion about pretty, popular girls is that some take it the wrong way; they think they deserve it or they are better than other people, so it makes them mean. Like one of our classmates, Janeen, who ended up still pretty-ish even at 30, but with a perpetual sneer on her face that pretty much cancelled out her perfect butt and expensive hair.

But some just give thanks for it every day, see it as a blessing and continue on their merry way. Their pretty loveliness transcending their dewy skin, making them even prettier as time goes on. Erica was kind of like this, she just expected to be pretty, loved it, enjoyed it, and voila! Life just eased her along like she was on some beautiful river.

Then there were the pretty popular girls like Geri Wellsley who never could figure out how she had gotten there. She used to confess to us that she secretly felt she didn't deserve it, but we would always assure her it was her personality that made her so well liked. Her own mother had been a jolly fat woman, sweet and smiling and wonderful but not traditionally pretty. Her dad had been tall and skinny and kind of dorky, though no one cared because he was so kind. Her sisters had been a little chubby and nothing special to look at, though so helpful and friendly everyone had liked them. Then along had come Geri, like a beautiful flower everyone had to admire, a shining beauty no one could ignore.

Geri explained, "I always felt how fleeting being pretty was, and as I've gotten older I've gotten chubbier and seen it slipping away from me. I wonder how much my looks have gotten me through my life. Fair or unfair, I couldn't help but witness how people treated me differently based on my looks. I was chosen as a cheerleader in high school over other girls who were more athletic and confident; I got my job as a receptionist despite having no training or education; Jason, pursued me and has always treated me well. Is it because I actually deserve it?"

I nodded, "Of course you do!"

Erica agreed, then considered, "I know what you mean. I hate thinking that way Geri. Don't even get me started! You aren't even half way as entitled as me. If my dad weren't Bruce Princeton would I even have a job at all?"

I had to pipe in here. "Hey! What about me? I don't have any of your good looks, Plain Jane sitting here. And I can safely say that, yes, it is definitely your beauty that has carried you easily through life!"

We all laughed as Erica poured more of the gold medal local wine.

"I've suspected this for a while now," Geri added, "but I hope not, because lately I've been really gaining weight. It started slowly at first, when Chloe was born, then after Simon it was more. But over the years it's crept up more and more and now I've reached a point where I can't even wear jeans anymore. When I first noticed the extra chubbiness I thought maybe it would just be a little silken layer, adding a little bit of fat to my face, making me look young."

Amanda agreed, "You definitely look young, your skin is great Ger."

"Yeah, well Jason even told me how pretty I looked at first, but now he doesn't mention my weight anymore at all. No one does. In fact, now people didn't really look at me much at all anymore. It's sad."

Erica patted her oldest friend on the arm, "I'm so sorry. I think you're beautiful no matter what."

I wasn't sure what to say. I wanted to make it better for Geri, to reassure her, but I didn't want to make her feel worse. I had a few friends who were in the same boat, though none really wanted to talk about their weight. I wondered if this was partially prompted by Erica visiting. Erica was constantly on a diet, she had to be considering how frequently she had her picture taken and how mean the tabloids would be to her if she got even slightly overweight. But as I watched my sister and our old friends I realized Erica was such a good friend, so pragmatic about the way she looked. She could laugh about her looks being her job. It just didn't matter that she was beyond amazing looking. I admired how she smoothly changed the subject; even though Erica was hurting, she could still sense that this was a sensitive subject for Geri. Being with Erica was like being a kid again. We talked about books and cooking and decorating, real things, things that made us happy. But every so often Erica would lapse back into a withdrawn sadness.

At the end of the evening Erica suggested a 7:00 am walk. Christina and Amanda both had plans, but Geri readily agreed.

"A walk!" Geri laughed, "I haven't so much as walked around the block in five years but if you need some fresh air I will humor you."

I agreed too, I was happy to see my little sister taking an interest in life.

So at seven the next morning, I called to Erica to hurry up, then I walked out and met Geri in front of our house. Geri had her small kids bundled into sweaters to combat the still chilly spring air. When I got outside she was doing squats, right there in the the front yard.

She laughed when I walked out the front door. "I didn't feel terrible, like I thought I would. In fact, I feel better than I have in days. Weeks. Years. Since I was on the cheer squad."

Her good cheer was infectious. I joined her in a couple of half-hearted squats, and by the time Erica came out we were both holding onto our aching thighs.

Erica laughed. "What happened to you! You look like you are inspired."

Geri smiled as she completed a final squat, "I think I might be. I'm sick of having no energy. I need to take my body back. Do you work out every day?"

Erica rolled her eyes, "Of course. If I don't my trainer will kill me when I get back. She gets me up at six every morning, rain or shine, and runs me all over the canyon. Why? Want to join me tomorrow too? How about if I'm your trainer! It'll keep me from wimping out."

Geri hesitated, but only for a minute, "Yes! Yes! I need this! I know you'll only be here a few days, but I need to get back on that horse. Your house or mine?"

I laughed, reluctantly agreeing. I wasn't too thrilled with my energy level either. I decided if my sister was back in town I might as well join her on her never-ending quest for greatness.

So with that decided we started out down tree-lined Palouse Street, trying to stay off the topic of unkind fans, noncommittal boyfriends, or funerals. It was cathartic for all of us and left me wondering if I could talk Erica into staying here for good.

Poor Normy

After saying good-bye to Geri we returned to our parents house where my mom was eager to show Erica her latest decorating project. As Angie and I sipped coffee, surreptitiously reading the paper while my mom chatted happily on, I tried to ignore the incessant banging from overhead. I could barely hear our mother explain to Erica how she was remodeling the kitchen and foyer. After giving Erica the background, describing the layers of wallpaper and hidden crown molding, the former movie star swept dramatically through the house to show off all she had accomplished on the 1907 downtown mansion.

Moms yipping Yorkshire Terriers, Norman and Maxine (who we secretly called Normal and Taxing) appeared underfoot to greet us. Of course in their exuberance they got all tangled in Erica's feet. As she backed, up looking up at the newly installed chandelier she stepped on Norman, the bigger of the two. Both Erica and Norman yelped as Erica attempted to right herself by grabbing a nearby ladder. Unfortunately, a full can of Coral Dream paint was partially open on the ledge of the ladder and, as the ladder wobbled, we all watched in horror as the can turned over, the contents spilling all over Erica. She managed to jump out of the way just in time to let Norman catch some of the paint. Both Erica and Norman were miserably dripping paint all over the impressive pine floor as Adelaide Princeton wailed, channeling her best 1980's romantic dramedy.

"Norman! My Normy, are you OK my little pooch?" She cooed, fluttering toward the little dog. Norman immediately shook off, spraying bits of Coral Dream all over the nearby wall and staircase. "Pick him up Erica, hon, he's terrified! Oh Normy!"

Angie quickly took action, dashing off to gather towels and other cleaning supplies.

Erica complied, mainly to stop her mother from shrieking. She seemed to be at that point of disaster where she didn't see how anything could get worse. I could see paint dripping down her face, puddling in her cleavage, her blue silky sweatshirt destroyed.

Just then, two men walked in. One, who was obviously the painter dressed in white overalls and a white cap, froze, gape mouthed at the sight of Erica and the little dog both covered in paint. The other was tall and broad shouldered, golden-skinned and dark-haired. Erica's face immediately changed when she saw him, her mouth falling open. I looked more closely at him and recognized him as Amanda's brother, Charlie Jones. I knew about Erica's long-standing interest in Charlie, and it was as if she were 10 years old again, secretly in love with the quiet musical boy from her fourth grade class, mutely staring at him. Charlie looked at her without seeing anything but the coral pink paint, his face registering shock at the disaster all over the floor and Erica.

Adelaide was very flustered, wanting to grab the wriggling, paint covered dog but not wanting to ruin her white silk blouse. Her hands fluttered around helplessly as she whimpered about her dog. Erica held the little Yorkie against her chest as she dipped her face into her shoulder to try to stop the paint from running into her eyes. I could tell she was fighting the urge to start crying, I imagined after the past two weeks of tears this didn't even seem worth getting upset over.

Charlie stepped forward and deftly solved the problem. Taking the dog from Erica and tucking him safely under one arm while simultaneously pulling a towel from his back pocket, he handed the towel to Erica.

"Thanks," she breathed gratefully, mopping the paint from her face. She could feel it start to harden as it dried on the back of her neck and forehead.

When she looked up at Charlie their eyes met and the effect was immediate, everything seemed to freeze and she felt herself tumbling into them. He furrowed his strong brow, seeming to recognize her but not sure from where. His deep dark brown eyes searching intently into hers, trying to identify why she seemed so familiar. Before they could speak he sprang to action.

"Is it water-based paint?" he asked the painter, who was clearly embarrassed and at a loss for how to help. The painter nodded quickly, eager to do anything to make the situation better.

Charlie managed to get the squirming dog wiped off enough to hand to Adelaide, then turned back to Erica. "If you get in the shower it should wash out pretty easily."

She felt her cheeks burn at the idea of discussing a shower with him and all she could manage was a scared nod. Slipping off the Keen sandals she had traveled in, she stepped over the puddle accumulating on the floor.

"Thanks, good idea, I'll - I'll go do that." She appeared too flustered to say anything more. Without looking back she sprinted up the stairs to her bedroom where her luggage was waiting for her.

Remember Me?

After a warm shower Erica seemed much calmer, most of the coral pink paint had washed off easily, only a small amount was still visible stuck in her hairline. She joined me where I was sitting at the kitchen counter, thumbing through the newspaper, waiting for her to come back downstairs. Her face free of makeup, she wore a cozy black cashmere sweats and black spaghetti-strap tank top. She had pulled her long hair into a damp bun and she swished downstairs in her sheepskin slippers. She joined me at the counter, taking a sip of my coffee and stealing the comics.

"Poor, poor Normy." I said, keeping my face serious.

She swatted me with a section of rolled up newspaper, laughing. "Thank goodness Taxing didn't get painted too, she'd probably still be running around getting little pink footprints all over the house. What ever possessed mom to buy those little rat-dogs?"

I shook my head. My mom loved dogs, we all did, but after her Standard Poodle, Snickerdoodle, had died two years ago she had surprised us with Norman and Maxine. Yorkshire Terriers have their charms, but after the intelligent and dignified Snickerdoodle, Erica and I were having a hard time accepting them.

We heard cheerful whistling, Charlie walked onto the outdoor patio with blueprints tucked under his arm. We could see him clearly through the double french doors, which were open wide to let in the beautiful spring day. He didn't notice us at first as he unrolled the plans and laid them on the table near the door. I almost greeted him but she stopped me with a look. She just wanted to watch him work. His dark eyebrows were pulled together in concentration, his brown eyes scanning the complex papers in front of him. He also had a tablet where he was jotting notes as he referenced his work. I chuckled and nudged her, she had harbored such a crush on Charlie Jones when she was young. He hadn't noticed her really, though she had mooned over him continuously. She had only revealed her crush to Geri and me, and in her childish way she had tried to even flirt with him.

I giggled to myself remembering a love letter she had written to him for Valentine's Day. After my own futile letter-writing campaign to Raymond, I had encouraged her to write a letter to Charlie. How she had poured over it, rewriting it until it was perfect, then when it was written on scented pink stationery in her best handwriting, asking Geri to deliver it. Geri had complied, carrying the precious love letter (what could it have said? I don't remember. Probably something like I like you, do you like me?) to Charlie as he came in from lunch. Geri had returned, breathless, to report that Charlie had told her to tell Erica that he thought Erica was cute! She was cute! Erica, Geri and I had freaked out over this proclamation for the rest of the day, the week! Eventually Amanda had wanted to know what was happening and when Erica revealed her secret crush on Amanda's brother, Amanda had been thrilled! She had been briefly convinced that they would be sisters-in-law and had wanted to tell him…but Erica had put a stop to that. I think the idea of actually having to talk to Charlie freaked her out because she never really talked about him after that.

And nothing had ever happened. It was just a few weeks after this that our parents good friends, Mr. and Mrs. Silverman, had come up to "quaint little Walla Walla" for a visit, taken one look at Erica's fresh blonde looks and had asked her to audition for Kids Rock. Our mother's voice had been well known during her movie star days and Erica did not disappoint, in fact her surprisingly deep and throaty voice had made her the one distinctive singer on the show, carrying her and Jimmy to fame.

Jimmy. Thinking of our friend, Erica's closest friend, brought a lump to my throat. How was Erica handling all this? I looked over at her and saw she was still staring at Charlie dreamily, a small smile on her lips. I chuckled, shaking my head. She snapped to attention and looked at me.

"What?"

"You. He's still really cute. Maybe you should write him a note. I can deliver it for you if you want." I joked.

Tossing her hair, she got up. "I am no longer twelve. I can do better than that."

Her movement alerted Charlie who turned and saw us in the kitchen, looking out at him. He straightened up and cleared his throat.

"I'm sorry, I didn't realize you were there…I needed to get these specs in before tomorrow so we can…."

He trailed off as she approached him, stepping outside into the morning sunlight. Taking two big steps toward her, he put his hand on her elbow. I could see her smiling up at him as he got near, though he stayed a respectful distance from her.

"Are you OK?" He asked quietly, looking closely at her. Once again the spark between them felt palpable, I felt embarrassed to be hearing their conversation. I started busying myself with tidying up the newspaper and dishes. I could still hear their conversation, though I tried to pretend I couldn't.

"I'm just, sad. My friend, I -" she tried to speak, but the intensity of the conflicting emotions was making her stammer. He guided her, his hand still on her elbow, to the bench by the door. Neither seemed concerned about me. I began noisily washing the breakfast dishes.

"Here, sit down. I heard about your friend. I'm sorry." He sat next to her and tilted his head to the side, looking carefully at her.

"Do you remember when we were in school together? And the few times I saw you in Portland?" He asked, but then realizing this may seem rude considering how upset she was, he quickly backpedaled, "I mean, you got so famous and left, but we were friends back then, I'm sure you have forgotten me. I remember you, I just…" He trailed off, clearly embarrassed and unsure how to continue.

She was no longer covered with pink paint, she was no longer an awkward twelve year old. This was Erica Princeton, world-famous rock star and she knew how to talk to men.

"Charlie, Charlie, Charlie, how could I have forgotten you? Oh, the agony of it! Here I traveled clear up here to Walla Walla just to see you and you think I just cold-heartedly forgot all about you?" She had shaken off her sadness and awkwardness in exchange for one of her favorite activities, being the charming star she had grown used to being.

Not sure if she was serious or teasing he haltered out a couple of unintelligible sounds, but before he could wonder any further, she burst out laughing. "OK, I'm exaggerating, I'm here to see my parents. But Charlie, of course I remember you." She was serious now, lowering her voice she continued, "you were kind of special to me."

He leaned closer to her, "What? What did you say?" He asked earnestly.

Looking up at him with her turquoise blue eyes, I'm sure he felt the intensity of her gaze. I could see her lean in to him, his arm resting against hers as he sat next to her on the bench.

This is where I excused myself, though neither seemed to hear me. Just as I was walking out I saw him touch her chin, tilting her head back so he could look into her demurely lowered eyes, "I think you may have said I was special to you. Well, Erica, you were special to me to. I still have that Valentine you wrote for me. No one else has ever been so genuinely sweet to me. I have thought about you ever since you left."

I scurried down the hall. How embarrassing to overhear that! But how wonderful too.

Just as I stepped out of the kitchen I saw our mother bustling toward me, a big smile on her face as she clutched Erica's cellphone like a trophy in front of her.

"Stop mom!" I whispered, trying to step in front of her.

She walked right past, entering the kitchen. I followed just in time to see Charlie giving Erica a sweet hug, her head resting against his chest.

"Erica! Malcolm for you!" Her mother's high-pitched voice, so sweet when she was calling someone down to dinner or cheering at a screening, was like shattering glass this time as it cut through their peaceful embrace.

Adelaide bustled into the kitchen, apparently unaware of the moment shared between her daughter and her contractor. "It's Malcolm! You left your phone on the sun terrace, so when I saw it buzzing for the third time I just took the liberty and -" she paused, looking between Erica and Charlie.

"Am I interrupting something?" She asked suspiciously as she handed Erica her phone.

"No, no, we were just catching up," began Erica as she found the phone suddenly at her ear, "Oh! Malcolm, how are you?"

Walking out into the hallway for privacy, I heard her voice instantly take on the anxious tone she seemed to always have with Malcolm.

"Yes," I could hear her saying,"I should be at the studio on Monday. Don't worry, the songs will be ready. I'll be working on them."

She clutched my arm as I tried to walk away, her eyes were pleading with me to help her. I didn't know how I could though.

"I know it's urgent Malcolm."

I couldn't help but notice that her "boyfriend" of three years didn't even bother asking about her trip or how she was coping.

Her voice wavered slightly, "A surprise? That…good. I hope it's good, right? And I am working on a special surprise, too."

And with that she pulled the phone away from her face and looked at it, shaking her head.

"He hung up." She said indignantly. "What did I ever see in that guy?" She asked me before tucking her phone away.

I shook my head, "I have no idea. He's charming, I give you that. Do you seriously plan to be there next week? After the way he acted at the funeral?"

She rolled her eyes. "Believe me, it is not for him. His company is the best and the guys and I have been working with them for a long time. We've been planning to record with them, I can't bail on Carlisle and Ben now."

Then her face brightened and she bit her lip. "So…did you get a load of Charlie?" She whispered, looking toward the kitchen.

I covered my face with my hands, laughing. "Probably more than you would have wanted! I'm sorry, I think I managed to take in that entire romantic moment."

She put her hands over her heart gleefully, a big smile filling her face. I followed her back into the kitchen where our mother was talking to Charlie. I nearly ran into her when she stopped abruptly, Addie was gushing on about Malcolm.

"And he's a music producer!" She was telling Charlie, whose brown eyes had lost their soft glow and were now deliberately not looking at Erica.

Erica cut our mom off, "Thanks mom," she said curtly, "I work with him. You know we broke up, right?"

Adelaide waved her manicured hand loftily. "Well, on-again, off-again may be your style, but I'm sure eventually you two will give me some more grandchildren."

And with that devastating proclamation, our mother sailed obliviously out of the kitchen, not seeing the pain she had caused to enter Charlie's eyes.

Out on the Town

That night our mom invited our entire Walla Walla family over for dinner. Erica and I were thrilled to see our cousin Chester with his wife Loreen and a little less pleased to see our slightly younger cousins Heather, Nicole, and Emily. Pearson and Perry disappeared into the game room to wait for Chester and Loreen's kids, Levi and Hadley, to show up.

Cousins can be both a blessing and a curse. Our cousins in Los Angeles, the daughters of our dad's brother, are easy to be around and close friends. Chester, too, has always been kind and he and his wife are a ton of fun. My other three cousins have been harder to accept. My mom and her younger sister, Antoinette, had a rivalry stretching their entire lives. Though they both smoochied and hugged and made a big spectacle about loving each other for photographs and celebrity interviews, we all knew better. Antoinette had followed Adelaide to Los Angeles and had also become famous, but as a singer. Like our mom, Aunt Etta had the good sense to retire young and return home. But now they spent their days bumping around their too-small hometown, competing with each other.

This would probably be comical, except Aunt Etta's daughters were just like her and directed all their wrath onto Erica. For years we had endured their ridicule and insults veiled under friendly banter. I usually just ignored them, it was easy considering they were so much younger than me. Besides, not one did much more with her life than live off of her mom's residual fame.

But on a night like tonight it looked like we were going to have to put up with our Walla Walla cousins. I was just glad both Angie and Loreen were going to be there, I knew both of them would gladly defend us against their subtle girl attacks. When Aunt Etta and the girls arrived I greeted them politely, leading them into the front living room. Mom's favorite housekeeper had stayed late and brought our drinks as we settled into the comfortable chairs and couch around the fireplace.

Etta clapped her hands together and asked Erica how her latest tour was going. Erica looked at the floor and quietly said she was taking a break, but would go back to recording soon.

Heather, the oldest, scowled at her, crossing her arms. "How can you record without Jim Jackson?"

Erica's eyes widened, "Well, I -"

Just then Angie came in carrying a tray of hors devours, "It will be a tribute of course. How is your program going Heather?" She said as she set down the tray.

Heather, who at twenty-five had been married and divorced three times (though without kids) had just started school to be a beautician. She had never held a job before, but I'd overheard Etta telling my mom she was tired of Heather complaining of being bored all the time. She needed a hobby, not to mention her trust fund was dwindling.

Heather shrugged, noncommittally. "It's too easy." She said with a sneer.

Nicole and Emily were sitting on the other side of the room, both engrossed by their phones. Nicole, at twenty-three, worked as a waitress on occasion, though she mainly just traveled, staying in fancy resorts, posting on social media. Twenty-one-year-old Emily had never worked or gone to school. All three sisters had different dads, Emily's dad paid as much attention to her as Nicole and Heather's dads, which is to say, none. But she was lucky because he had been a professional football player and gave her an enormous allowance. Though Emily was pretty, I suspected her silence covered up her vacant mind. She was kind when she was alone, but was willing to follow whatever mean scheme Nicole or Heather suggested. I suspected her older sisters used her to bankroll their frequent Vegas and Hawaii trips.

Our dad walked in with our mom on his arm. Her older brother August trailed behind with our Aunt Lacey. Everyone snapped to attention and smiled as they walked in, Erica and me because August and Lacey give our family the normalcy we all need and we love to be around them. I suspect Etta and my cousins have an ulterior motive: August still runs our grandparents wheat ranch along with their son Chester. With the way my aunt and her daughters burn through money I'm sure they have no qualms about hitting her big brother up for the occasional loan or handout.

"Auggie! Lace!" Aunt Etta exclaimed jumping up to give hugs all around. As she returned to her perch on the love seat she hissed at Nicole and Emily to put their phones away and join us. Both reluctantly did.

Chester and Loreen arrived twenty minutes late, as was usual. Once Chester was there it really began to feel like a party. Everyone's favorite, August and Lacey's son Chester greeted everyone with a big smile. He had been a football player in college before returning home to run the family farm. His easy laugh and friendliness towards everyone made him the life of any party. Loreen had taken some getting used to. She was from a small town in Eastern Oregon and hadn't seemed like she would fit in at first. My mom called her low-brow when she first met her, and I guess that could describe her. She smokes, shamelessly lighting up with complete disregard to the fact that just about everyone hates smoking. She cusses. She tosses back shots, plays on a pool league, and dyes her hair white blonde.

I'll admit, it took me a little while to get used to her too. But over the years I have come to appreciate her honesty and good nature. Compared to the sullen sneers of Heather, Nicole, and Emily, I would much rather be with Loreen. It's no surprise that the three younger cousins are scornful of Loreen. As soon as she walked into the room I saw Nicole look at Emily and roll her eyes, shaking her head and fingering her own lapel. I looked at Loreen. Sure enough, she had a gold butterfly pinned to her lapel. I guess it was a little big, but not terrible. Looking back at Emily and Nicole I could see Emily laughing and shaking her head.

When we sat down to dinner, the first thing Nicole said was, "I love your pin, Loreen."

Loreen looked down at the butterfly pin and smiled, "Oh isn't that cute? I found it at the antique shop last week."

Emily dissolved into silent giggles, covering her mouth. Nicole and Heather looked at each other and smirked. Loreen glanced at each of them then met my gaze. I shook my head slightly, we were used to these types of exchanges. Loreen was a champion at fighting back, though. She didn't even hesitate, just smiled and asked Nicole why she wasn't getting her roots touched up.

Erica, who was sitting next to me, kept her face passive, but I heard her sniff out a quick laugh. She and I were both total wimps at dealing with mean girls, but watching women like Loreen and Angie was an inspiration.

After dinner we went to a new dance club that had opened downtown, Nicole's idea. The loud music and flashing lights gave me an instant headache and I quickly joined Loreen and Erica in the bathroom.

"Ugh! I am way too old for this!" I said, sweeping my hair up off my neck to cool off.

Erica and Loreen both seemed happy to be there. "It's fun, Penny." Erica said, pulling lipstick out of her tight jeans. "Just forget how old you are and get out there and dance."

"I suppose I could try," I said. "It's been years since I did this.

When we emerged we saw our cousins sitting at a dark table across the room. Heather, Nicole, and Emily had pink drinks in front of them and were all scrolling through their phones. I hadn't noticed before, but all three were wearing almost exactly the same outfit: black jeans, a silky black tank top, and black spiky heels. It looked weird. I wondered if Heather picked the outfit out and then told the other two what to wear. Heather wanted a picture with Erica, whipping out the camera and leaning back with their faces pressed together before Erica had a chance to say anything. Erica complied, but I could tell she was annoyed. Not one of the cousins had even spoken to her yet this evening, they had purposefully left her out of any conversation they were having, and now Heather would post a picture on Twitter or Facebook or somewhere saying what a great time she was having with the famous Erica Princeton. She did the same thing every time they were together.

Erica always tried, though, I could give her that. Turning to the three sisters, who were now huddled around Heather's camera, probably deciding which picture made Heather look the best and adding a filter.

"Come on girls! Let's go dance!" She hollered cheerfully over the indecipherable music. "You too, Chester."

Loreen jumped up. Chester held up his full beer and yelled that he'd probably join us after he finished. I reluctantly got up.

Erica was a phenomenal dancer. I could tell she was trying to tone it down, to not draw attention to herself, but years of dance lessons and performing gave her a star power that no one could ignore. Her long blonde hair was loose, swinging over her bare shoulders, and the black dress she had chosen showed off her legs.

I was surprised to see Charlie Jones sitting across the room staring at her. She hadn't see him yet, but I could tell he was pretty happy she was there. I saw he was with a big group of guys and saw one with a button that said 'Groom.' Ha ha, a Bachelor Party! I looked more closely and recognized a few guys from school and waved.

Charlie cheerfully waved back and stumbled over with two of his friends, Dave and Chris, to say hi. Dave and Chris seemed thrilled when Erica remembered them and gave out hugs. When she saw Charlie she walked confidently toward him.

I heard her yell, "I was hoping I'd see you. Now I'm ready for a great night!" She smiled.

I could see him softening towards her, though his face was still suspicious, I imagined he might still be thinking of Malcolm. But he seemed to relax when she grabbed his hand and invited him to dance. We all had a lot of fun, dancing to overly loud music I didn't recognize. Chester joined us soon after, though Heather, Nicole, and Emily never did. In fact on occasion I could hear them shrieking about how embarrassed they were that we were dancing.

At one point the music stopped just for a moment allowing Emily's high-pitched voice to be heard clearly, "Oh my gah! Why does Erica always have to dance?"

I met Erica's eye and shrugged my shoulders. I could tell it hurt her to know our cousins were talking about her, even if their conversation was foolish. I got mad. Here she was, trying to heal from the loss of one of her closest friends, and these silly girls can't do anything but ridicule her for…dancing? At a dance club? Still looking at Erica, I started walking towards them. I'm sure my face showed that I was going to say something to defend her. But she quickly shook her head, then she raised her eyebrows toward Charlie, who was still dancing with her. They looked really cute together.

I had admire her ability to brush off their mean comments. It had gone on all evening, though everything was so subtle no one but Loreen had noticed. Tiny little jabs designed to make Erica feel bad about herself.

"Oh they wouldn't have heard of you Erica, they listen to popular music."

"Two glasses of wine already Erica?"

"Oh you had to have been there."

"Oh you know, Erica, back when people knew who you were."

It was endless, but all delivered with a friendly smile, sweetly. And then the eye contact and tiny giggles any time Erica said anything. When Uncle Auggie asked about her remodeled kitchen and described it, all three girls had laughed when she said it was like 'The Brady Bunch'. But then claimed to be laughing about something one had said that no one else heard. By the time we had arrived at the club I was pretty much ready to write them off, maybe pretend I didn't know who they were.

But Erica held her head high and ignored them, which seemed to make them even more angry. Yet, they were too insecure to even stand up to dance, just sitting at the dark table looking at their phones and talking to each other. After an hour Erica said she needed some air and suggested we go outside. The guys from the bachelor party hollered that they wanted to go hear a band at a place down the street, so we left.

I was hoping the sisters would stay behind, but Chester invited them and they tagged along after us. When we got outside and started walking Erica, holding Charlie's arm, looked up at him and with a big smile sang along with the dance song drifting out after us.

"Put your hands in the air if you just don't care!" Charlie clearly thought she was cute, putting the hand not holding her up in the air.

Heather couldn't stand it though. "Why does she always have to sing?"

Emily laughed loudly, "I know, she's embarrassing."

They weren't even trying to hide the fact that they were unkindly discussing Erica right in front of her. I was done, I stopped walking and stood in front of them, blocking their path on the sidewalk.

"You are not welcome to join us for the rest of the night." I said. Even though I had worked at learning to stand up for myself, I could still feel my heart beginning to pound.

Emily got a look of confusion on her face, "Wha?" she said, leaving her mouth open.

Nicole and Heather, on the other hand, understood immediately, and were prepared to fight.

"Who are you to decide if we are welcome?" asked Heather.

"Yeah, nobody cares what you say." Nicole said, wrinkling her nose and looking me up and down.

My heart was beating so fast I could barely breathe. I feared if I tried to speak I would stutter, but I took a deep breath and spoke slowly.

"You are being mean and I don't want to be around you." Was all I could get out before turning back around. I was pleasantly surprised to see Loreen standing right behind me. Erica, Charlie, Chester, and all the bachelor party guys were halfway up the block, unaware of our little tiff.

"Go away. Come back when you can act like grown ups."
Loreen said, totally calm and strong. "No one wants to hear you
knock Erica."

Her strength gave me courage. "It's obvious you're jealous.
Who wouldn't be? But it just makes you seem mean. You are
better than that."

I could tell that I had hit a nerve. Nicole and Emily both
looked at the ground, though I thought for a moment Heather
might start yelling insults at me. Then she thought better of it
and shrugged.

"Well, you guys can be mean too." Heather said, "You
always leave us out. You never even invite us to do anything."

And with that she spun around, Nicole and Emily right
behind her.

By the time Loreen and I reached the little bar, Chester was
yawning and hinting at wanting to go. I could have left too, but
when I looked for Erica I saw her tucked into a cozy corner of
the patio, talking with Charlie. Their heads were close together
and they both looked so happy, I didn't want to interrupt quite
yet. When I pointed them out, Chester and Loreen agreed to stay
for a little longer. We managed to find a table in the crowded
bar with our friend Amanda, Charlie's sister. I was surprised to
see she was there with her parents.

"What are you doing here?" I leaned over to ask her.

"I texted you! Don't you check your phone? Charlie called
me this afternoon and said the guys from the band asked him to
join them for a couple of songs. They work for him sometimes."

We sat down and enjoyed the band and a few minutes later
the lead singer called out for Charlie to come up and join them.
He jumped up and ran up to the stage, taking the microphone.
Erica joined us, clearly thrilled to be watching Charlie play.

"Was this planned?" I asked her as Charlie tested the mic and the guitar.

"Well, yes, but I thought they were teasing him. I knew he used to play music but I didn't realize he still did."

The band, which had been very good before, was even better with Charlie up there with them. He was a skilled guitarist and had a clear deep baritone voice that mixed nicely with the rest of the band for the two songs he played. It helped that his friends from the bachelor party were loudly cheering him on.

Once the band finished playing Erica decided we should all walk back to our parents house, so we could continue the concert. Pulling out her two spare guitars, she handed one to Charlie. Chester, Loreen, and the guys from the bachelor party drank beer and played pool in the game room while we enjoyed listening to them play. Charlie accompanied her on the guitar and softly harmonized with her rich alto voice. I couldn't help but think of Jim, who had been such a good creative partner for Erica. I knew no one would or could ever replace him, but it made me happy to see my sister playing music again. I saw her meet his eye while they were playing and I could tell they were sharing a deep connection.

While Loreen was regaling us with a wild story about being spotted by a bear while picking berries the summer before I noticed they had stopped playing. I glanced over and saw Charlie leaning toward Erica, giving her a tender kiss. I wasn't the only one who saw. His friends Chris and Dave saw too and immediately started whistling. They pulled away, laughing, but I could tell they were both really happy.

As everybody left a few minutes later I saw him give her another quick kiss and ask if he could see her again soon.

She gave him a hug. "Of course! You'd better call me tomorrow Charlie Jones!"

The Wrong Guy

The next day was Sunday and Pearson and Perry and I were up early. Erica only had two more days to visit and my boys were eager to hang out with their aunt. My mom had organized another family event, brunch, and the boys wanted to visit with her before everyone else came. Pearson had brought out his guitar and wanted to show her a song he was writing, Perry had a soccer ball under his arm. Both stood expectantly looking up the stairs towards the direction of her room. My dad and I chuckled, wondering which one would get my sister first.

She came downstairs, humming happily. I thought I recognized one of the improvisational song she had played the night before with Charlie. As the two boys gathered around her, clamoring for her attention, my mom wondered aloud why they didn't want her attention that much.

"I think it's because you aren't a rock star, Addie my love." My dad said as he grabbed his briefcase. He was headed out the door to his downtown office. Though he didn't work on as many projects now that he was semi-retired, he still went to his beautiful office overlooking Main Street each morning. He was currently writing a screenplay with one of his friends from Los Angeles.

Just as he reached the front hallway the doorbell rang. I saw Erica perk up, looking away from Perry and Pearson, eagerly talking over each other describing soccer and music simultaneously to both her and Angie. I could tell she thought it might be Charlie by the look of hope on her face.

But it was not Charlie on our parents spacious front porch. Instead we could see Malcolm peering into the house around our dad, looking awkward and overdressed in a Brooks Brother's suit. Our dad didn't smile, taking in Malcolm's smarmy good looks and too big smile with the understanding of someone who has spent a long time dealing with wheeler-dealers in Hollywood. With a curt nod he stepped around Malcolm, pausing only briefly to look down his nose at the shorter man as he passed by him before continuing down the porch steps.

Malcolm entered the foyer, closing the large front door behind him. He appeared nervous and guilty. He saw Erica, standing in front of me and grabbed her hand. He looked her deeply in the eyes, saying huskily.

"I'm sorry I tried to push you. You clearly needed a break. You look calmer, more relaxed."

She softened, smiling slightly. "Yes, this has been really good for me. I need time to grieve, I need to be with people who care about me."

He nodded quickly. "Of course you do. Take all the time you need. All that matters is that you feel better."

I could see Erica beginning to open up to him again, he was speaking in a low tone and she was stepping closer to him. He now held her hand to his chest.

"So how's the song coming along?" He asked, still gazing into her eyes. From where I stood a few feet away I could see a little understanding flash across Erica's face, maybe she would finally see what a jerk he was being.

"I'm not ready to write anything yet. Like you said, I need time."

He laughed, dropping her hand abruptly, changing his tone.

"Well, yeah, but you can whip out a song. It's not like it really matters that much. Right babe? It's just a song?"

Erica's face registered the realization that all Malcolm really cared about was selling songs.

"Do you mean, since Jim is gone we have to get a song done quickly?" She asked slowly, looking at him carefully.

"Exactly! We have to ride this wave while it's at its biggest!" Malcolm said, his eyes snapping with enthusiasm. "The whole world is interested in the Jim Jackson scandal. Now is our chance to really rake it in. I knew you'd understand."

Erica's eyes narrowed. "Yes Malcolm, I understand. I understand that you care more about money than you do about me."

Was she speaking up for herself? I couldn't believe it! Not only did she seem to finally have come to her senses about what a jerk Malcolm could be, but she was also standing up to him. I was so proud of her!

But Malcolm was better than I thought. Not one to let a great catch like Erica just slip away in a fit of anger, he quickly smoothed over the situation.

"No, no! Not at all, you misunderstand me Erica. Of course people want to hear about Jim, but because they care about him. They care about you and the rest of the band."

His eyes were all soft and intense, staring into hers, and I was shocked when I could see she was falling for it. I wanted to jump in there and stop her from being charmed by this jerk anymore! But I couldn't, I had to just stand there and watch her nod, somehow forgetting that less than a minute before he had been talking about "raking it in." Ugh.

The Rivalry

Just at that moment, I looked out the front window and I saw Charlie pulling up in his beat up truck. He jumped out eagerly and began striding toward the house. He had flowers!

"Erica." I said, but my sister was smiling up at Malcolm, nodding.

"Erica!" I repeated louder.

She snapped to attention and looked at me. I nodded toward the front window where we could see Charlie coming up the steps, his face eager and cheerful. Erica lit up, but then quickly clouded as she looked over at Malcolm, still staring at her plaintively.

"This is important Malcolm." She said, "And no. I can't have it done by next week. Stop trying to smooth talk me."

And with that she stepped toward the door to open it, smiling and exclaiming "Charlie!" before stepping out onto the porch and closing the door behind her.

Alone with Malcolm in the foyer, I looked him up and down, not bothering to hide my dislike. I had liked him when Erica had first introduced us. But over the years he had shown that he cared more about himself than Erica, he cared more about money than Erica, he cared more about Erica's career than Erica - and I was tired of it.

He smiled at me, clearly about to try to charm me too. "So Penelope, Erica tells me you designed the costumes for her most recent show?"

He was good, I had to give him that. His sweet smile and penetrating gaze almost sucked me in for a second as I considered talking about my project. But I caught myself.

I nodded curtly. "Yes." I wasn't going to help him at all.

He searched around for something else to talk about.

"How are your boys? They are both in school now, Erica tells me. She is such a proud auntie." I was about to respond, determined to keep things pleasant but cold, when Malcolm looked out at the porch. At first he must have thought Charlie was inconsequential, but now his eyes narrowed as he looked out the small window and could see Erica standing close to Charlie on the porch.

He strode to the door and opened it, stepping outside. I followed him, arriving in time to hear Erica, holding a colorful bouquet of peonies, laugh and say, "See you tonight then."

Malcolm, sensing a rival, stood too close to Erica, and thrust his hand out toward Charlie.

"Malcolm Jamison Smithe." He practically shouted.

Charlie was clearly not impressed. Looking at Malcolm in his stiff blue suit and slick hair, Charlie only nodded his head curtly.

"Are you sure you have time to get together tonight, Erica?" Charlie asked, still looking at Malcolm.

Erica appeared calm, pleased by both visitors. But I knew her well enough to know she was anxious, and I hoped she was wishing Malcolm would go away. I decided to step in and try to help her out.

"Malcolm," I said, stepping forward. "I'm sure my mom will want to hear about the latest recording session for the group. Please come in."

Barely acknowledging me, he stepped even closer to Erica and put his arm proprietarily around her shoulder.

"Sorry, I traveled a long way to see Erica." Malcolm sneered at Charlie, looking down at him as he stood on the sidewalk in front of the house. "She told me she would have dinner with me tonight, so we can catch up and plan."

Charlie's face grew even stormier as her contemplated this. Before either had a chance to say anything, Erica ducked out from under Malcolm's arm and said, "Malcolm! We hadn't discussed anything. I didn't even know you were coming!"

But the thing was, this was Erica here, and her years of being polite and allowing our dad or Angie or Samantha or Jim or anyone else stand up for her had left her unprepared to stand up for herself. Her voice was too quiet, polite, even though I could tell from her red neck that she was truly angry.

Just at that moment our mom came prancing out.

"Malcolm! What a pleasant surprise!" She said, giving him a quick kiss on the cheek.

Turning to see Charlie, still awkwardly standing on the sidewalk, Adelaide said. "Oh hello Charlie. We weren't expecting any work done today. Will you come back Monday?"

Charlie wasn't even aware that Erica was upset, all he saw was a girl he had barely started talking to again with another guy on her parent's front porch. With a sad shrug, he looked at Erica before turning on his heel and stalking back to his truck.

"Charlie!" Erica called, but he didn't turn around.

Once we were back in the house, Malcolm pretended nothing had happened. He showered all his charm on our mom, oohing and aahing over every little detail of the house - which, in three years of dating he had never once visited. Erica was quiet and anxious, staying behind to watch Charlie drive off.

"I can't believe this." She said, tears welling in her eyes. "Yes, he has been really helpful with the band. But I am done! I don't want Charlie to think I'm with him. Oh Penny! Why is it so hard for me to stand up for myself?"

As our mother's tinkling laughter flowed out of the kitchen, I shook my head. "I'm just as bad. We're both just too nice for our own good."

Erica laughed a sad laugh. "Funny, I scream out grrrrl power lyrics on stages for thousands of fans…but I can't even stand up to Malcolm?"

"Yes you can Erica," I told her. "Just pretend you're Angie. Or Dad!"

Squaring her shoulders, she turned toward the kitchen. "Your are right! Look out world, I'm done being bossed around!"

But when she entered the kitchen, Addie, Pearson, Perry, and Angie were listening raptly as Malcolm was talking in his booming voice.

"The Raven is really excited to meet Erica, she's a big fan." He was saying.

Erica stopped, looking back at me. The Raven?

Erica and I had idolized The Raven our entire lives. A huge star since our childhood, she still consistently managed to pump out amazing albums. One of Erica's lifelong dreams was to meet her. A few years earlier their manager had delivered the message that The Raven was a fan of The Flying Foes and had been working with them to collaborate. So far only Jim had ever met her. Jim, The Raven, and three other big stars had performed a special Super Bowl half-time show two years before. Erica had been pretty hurt that the producers hadn't asked her and the whole group, but she understood that they had only selected one person from each band…and Jim was often seen as the face of The Flying Foes.

Malcolm turned to Erica, smiling his disarmingly handsome smile. He reached for her, as if he expected her to just nestle into him. She shook her head slightly, still obviously annoyed. But his reference to The Raven had intrigued her.

"I couldn't wait to tell you, Erica. I had planned a special dinner for you so I could reveal my big surprise."

I snorted, yeah right. He always had some romantic thing he had planned to do for Erica but just somehow didn't follow through with.

Our mom clapped her hands. "Can you believe Malcolm arranged for you, Ben, and Carlisle to record an album with her!" Her face was all lit up with excitement. I wondered if it was because she genuinely liked The Raven or if she was just thrilled that her little sister's biggest rival from the past was superseding her.

Malcolm smiled demurely. "That's right, Erica, dear. I know how The Raven is a huge fan of The Flying Foes, so with our tragedy I called her and asked if she wanted to make a tribute album with you. She is about to set out on tour but has time next week. That's why I've been pressuring you to move so fast to finish up the songs."

Erica was clearly torn. She had always loved The Raven and had dreamed of working with her. But she was also angry at Malcolm. Glaring at him, I could see her trying to stay mad. But Pearson and Perry were bursting in with excited questions about the recording session, about the songs, about whether they could go too. I could see Erica relenting.

"Fine," she said, her jaw set in determination. "But Malcolm, you and I are done. I don't want to see you tonight or any night."

And with that uncharacteristically strong proclamation, she spun around and left, leaving Malcolm gaping after her.

Brunch

I found her a few minutes later, she was sprawled across the window seat overlooking the Weeping Willow tree, poking furiously at her cell phone. She looked up at me, still scowling, but her face relaxed when she realized it was me and not our mom or Malcolm there to scold her.

"That was pretty good Erica." I said, sitting down on the seat, moving her feet over to make room.

She looked at me with faint triumph in her face. "Really? You couldn't tell I was shaking?"

I shook my head. "Not at all. You were very strong. I'm proud of you."

She smiled slightly. "I'm trying to get ahold of Charlie, but he hasn't returned my texts."

I held out my hand for her phone. "Texts?" I raised my eyebrows at her. We had a rule that we never sent a guy two texts in a row. If he was so busy he couldn't respond after one text, then maybe he needed to find someone less special to date. Or something. It was something she had to work on often with Malcolm who had often made her wait days before responding to simple texts like how are you? or what are you doing this weekend?

She handed me the phone, a guilty smile on her lips. "OK, I may have broken the two-text rule. But the first text just said I'm sorry. I sent a second right after that said I'm still expecting to have dinner with him tonight. So that isn't really like two texts, more like one with a P.S."

I nodded grudgingly, "OK, I'll allow it. You don't look pathetic - yet. Just, no more!"

She promised. Then I reminded her that Aunt Etta, Uncle August, and everyone else would be over soon.

Erica sighed. "Do I really have to deal with the girls right now? Last night was brutal. Did you hear them laughing at me when we were dancing? And Heather and Nicole kept making fun of my shoes. My shoes!"

She picked up the beautiful wedge sandal she had worn the night before and looked at it. "Is there something strange or inappropriate about these shoes?" She asked me.

I shook my head, snorting. "The opposite. You know those shoes are beautiful. Those insecure girls will pick someone apart if they are even slightly threatened by her. It's terrible."

She nodded sadly. "I try to be kind, but it doesn't seem worth it. I tried to ask Emily about her latest Vegas trip and she hardly even answered. Then when I stood up she immediately started laughing with Heather and Erica. It's hard to pinpoint, but they just aren't kind. I was glad when they didn't join us at the second place. That was so fun, they would have just put a big damper on it."

I admitted how I had told them they weren't welcome to join us.

Her eyes widened. "No! You actually said that?"

"Yes, they wouldn't stop with their mean comments and I couldn't stand it. Loreen backed me up."

Erica high-fived me. "Good going!"

I looked at the ground. "I'm not sure, though. I felt bad because the last thing Heather said was how we leave them out and never invite them to do anything."

Erica furrowed her brow. "Is that true?"

I shrugged. "It might be. Well, it is, yes. But I never want to invite them, it's just too stressful when they are around."

She got a thoughtful expression. "I wonder what would happen if we tried to get to know them on our own, without the big group all the time? You know, like if I just invited Heather to lunch or something."

I cringed a little at the idea, but realized she probably had a point. "I suppose you are probably right. I've tried ignoring them for the past few years. But maybe you have the right idea. But I also think you should stand up for yourself if they're rude."

"Point taken." She said. "It sounds like we have battle plan: we'll be polite. I'll focus on being friendly to Heather and maybe you can see if Nicole wants to hang out or something."

"And if they're mean you won't just passively ignore it?" I reminded her.

"Right. I am prepared. No more Erica Princeton, door mat!"

Heather, Nicole, and Emily all came with Aunt Etta. I had imagined they would, although it had occurred to me that my outburst the night before might keep them away. But there they were, I think they actually enjoy the drama and confrontation. Although Aunt Etta was full of cheerful greetings, her daughters didn't even look up from their phones when we walked in. Taking a deep breath, I decided Erica had a point. Regardless of how they treated us, we were still polite. And maybe if we could just divide and conquer they would stop being so unkind as a group.

"Hi Heather! Hi Nicole! Hi Emily!" I said brightly, hoping I didn't sound overly chirpy. I sat right down on the chair next to Nicole. She looked up, seeming surprised to see me, but then right back to her phone.

"How are you this morning?" I asked her, unable to think of anything else to talk about.

She looked confused. "Me?"

"Well, yes, how are you? Are you having a good day?" I asked kind of lamely. This might not be a very good idea. I already felt weird.

I saw Nicole slide her eyes toward her older sister, who was sitting in another nearby seat. But Erica was perched on the ottoman in front of Heather's chair, cheerfully chatting with her. Finding that Heather wasn't available to share a silent eye-conversation about me, Nicole next swung her eyes to her younger sister. I could tell Emily, who was sitting on the other side of me, was now eagerly listening to me as I attempted to connect with my cousin.

I sat and patiently waited, still looking at Nicole. Was she even going to answer? Finally she seemed to register that I had asked her a polite question and ignoring me just made her look rude.

"Oh." She said curtly. "I'm fine."

Then she went back to her phone. I couldn't tell what she was doing, but it looked like she was sending a text message. Just after she stopped typing I heard Emily burst out laughing. Were they texting each other? I felt at a loss, I just didn't understand why they had to always act like this.

Erica was still sitting near Heather, smiling and nodding. Although Erica looked cheerful and relaxed, Heather was tense, sitting up very straight with her lips pressed together. It occurred to me that, although Erica might feel bad about our cousin's rude treatment, as long as Erica maintained her polite dignity only

Heather looked mean or unhappy. I decided to follow my sister's lead.

I focused my attention back at my other two cousins and tried again. "So, do you guys have any new trips coming up?" I asked Nicole, but also turning to look at Emily.

I could tell Nicole was considering not answering me, she looked around as if trying to figure out how to escape, but Loreen and Chester, leaning against the counter talking with all or our parents, must not have looked like a good respite.

She grudgingly answered. "Yes, New York."

I grasped at this. "How fun! Do you have tickets for any shows?"

Nicole's expression was still bored, she wouldn't look me in the eye. "Yeah, I think mom got something. I don't know."

Emily just sat silently, staring at us like I was stupid.

I couldn't keep trying to do this, they weren't giving me any help. Glancing at Erica, I could she was having about the same level of luck. Heather was checking her phone, shrugging at a question Erica was asking.

But I still persisted. "Well that sounds great, I bet you'll have fun."

Neither answered. I heard Nicole's phone buzz, she picked it up and stifled a giggle. Then she punched a few buttons and set it back down. Heather then looked down at her own phone, shook her head, and looked over at Nicole.

Erica looked at me. This was hopeless. I considered just addressing the issue directly. Saying something like, why are you being so unfriendly? Or just pointing out that I was trying to have a conversation and she was being rude. But instead I just opted to ignore it, pretend it didn't bother me, continue being polite while my cousins treated me and my sister with contempt.

When had this started? I could hardly remember, it had gone on so long. When we were really young they had idolized us. And being older, we had enjoyed their attention, though we hadn't ever really socialized with them. I'm five years older than Heather, really too old to ever have been her friend. But when we were younger Aunt Etta would come to Walla Walla from Los Angeles and I used to take Heather downtown and out to lunch. Nicole came with us a few times, too. By the time Emily was born I was nine. I was happy to hold Emily and I thought she was adorable, but pretty soon I was caught up in my own life.

I wonder if I was just a selfish teen and young adult and didn't pay attention to my cousins when they needed me to? I tried to remember, maybe there was some situation similar to the current brunch when they were trying to get my to play or pay attention to them and I was just caught up in my own life. It's certainly possible. Not to mention, by the time I moved back to Walla Walla I was married and had babies.

I continued sitting there, between my two young cousins, who were now furiously engaged in their phones. I thought about our past, how we had never really had a chance to get to know each other. I thought of their anger at Erica, how Erica had been so busy she probably had never thought to do anything special for them. I looked at the three of them, so obviously unhappy, and I just felt sorry for them.

I decided it didn't matter if they were rude or dismissive. I didn't have to engage in their games. I had never purposefully hurt them and I didn't have to be rude now. I would just continue being polite, ask the same polite questions I would ask anyone else, and not worry about these miserable girls.

I got up and said cheerfully, looking at both Nicole and Emily. "It's been good catching up," I said before walking over to the kitchen.

As we ate breakfast, Aunt Etta was regaling us with stories about her new Facebook page. "I wasn't sure at first. I thought it was just for the young people. I see my girls on Facebook all day and I thought I would never be able to figure out something so complex."

My parents both laughed, they refused to do any social media so far.

Heather chimed in, "But now you're on it more than any of us!"

Emily groaned, "Yeah mom, it's embarrassing. I can't post anything without you commenting or Liking it."

Aunt Etta looked confused. "But don't you want people to comment? And you three are obsessed with that little Like button. I swear, they have some type of competition going."

I could tell she was saying something her daughters weren't too excited for her to share. Nicole started to interrupt but Etta just barged on, unaware.

"This morning they were so excited! Erica, that little picture you and Heather took got hundreds of likes! Heather even had someone want to buy the rights to it so he could sell it to a magazine."

My mom was surprised. "People have such different ideas about entertainment these days! In our day no one wanted to see informal pictures of the stars. They wanted to see us looking glamorous."

Etta responded, but I wasn't really listening. I was looking at Erica. She was pretty good at hiding her emotions, but the picture thing bothered her, I could tell. It bothered me too. Our cousins were so rude to her, yet they still took pictures with her and shared them and tried to impress other people because they knew her. At least they didn't act fakey-nice though, so they could try to get more from her. Erica had encountered a lot of people like that. At least I had to give my cousins credit for being the genuine brats they always were.

After breakfast we all went out to the patio. Erica was sitting with our mom and Aunt Etta while Chaz and Loreen and I looked at the garden with my dad, August, and Lacey. Heather, Nicole, and Emily were sitting on the patio steps, deep in conversation. I looked up from dad's tomato plants to see Erica brushing tears off her cheeks. She was shaking her head and our mom and Aunt Etta were both patting her. I was glad to see her getting some comfort, losing Jim would be something she would need a long time to mourn.

I glanced at my cousins and was shocked to see that both Heather and Nicole were aiming their camera's at her. They were taking her picture!

"Hey!" I yelled, walking toward them.

They both immediately put their cameras down, looking guilty.

Everyone else looked at me like I was crazy.

"They were taking your picture, Erica." I told my sister, trying to keep calm. I couldn't believe it, I could just imagine how much a tabloid or gossip magazine would love to print pictures of the great Erica Princeton having a breakdown. The former actress Adelaide Princeton and the former singing sensation Antoinette Richardson flanking her would make it that much more valuable. But were my cousins really that bad off financially? My mom had mentioned their trust funds were dwindling, but stooping to this level was pretty low.

Erica's face reddened. I could see she was debating whether or not to speak. First she looked at my dad, but he was still talking to Chester and August about the garden. He probably didn't even have his hearing aid in. Then she looked into the kitchen where Angie was making phone calls. With just a look she knew she could get her assistant out here to yell at her cousin. But then I saw her set her jaw and sit up straighter. Was she going to defend herself?

"Heather, Nicole," she said softly. "I don't want you to take my picture. I need you to delete any pictures of me on your cameras."

Both sisters got red. I could see them exchange a brief look, as if they were considering lying. But then our mom got involved.

"Do you have a lot of pictures of Erica?" She asked.

Aunt Etta, still not grasping the severity of the situation, laughed. "Oh you should see some of the shots they got last night!"

Nicole was shaking her head, probably hoping her mom would shut up. But Etta had always been silly and she didn't even notice.

"It looks like you all had such a fun night! Erica dancing, a whole bunch of men from what looked like a bachelor party, they even showed me one of you getting pretty close with that contractor."

My mom nearly forgot about the pictures as she jumped on this information. "Contractor? Do you mean Charlie?" She looked at Erica, but Erica wasn't paying attention to her.

Instead Erica was out of her seat and striding furiously over to her cousins. She held out her hand, demanding the phones.

"Give them to me." She said firmly. I was proud of her, she never spoke this way.

Both Heather and Nicole looked like they were going to refuse, but at this point our dad had finally realized something was going on. He walked over with August, Chester, and Loreen.

As everyone watched them, Heather and Nicole reluctantly handed over their phones. Then they had to sit awkwardly, without their phones to distract or save them, as everyone scrolled through their pictures. They had so many unflattering pictures of Erica. Pictures of her dancing, but from an angle that made her butt look huge. Pictures where she was eating, scratching her nose, making strange facial expressions. And, after I had asked them to leave, they had followed us. There were even pictures of Erica sharing a sweet kiss with Charlie at the second bar.

Our dad was livid. He got absolutely silent and went into Mr. Hollywood Producer mode. He confiscated the phones and said he would ensure every incriminating photograph was absolutely deleted. He extracted a promise from both sisters that they had not done anything with the photographs yet. And he promised them that if any appeared in public he personally would take legal action. He didn't care if they were family.

Everyone else was mad too. Even Aunt Etta, who normally didn't worry about much more than what people were wearing or whether or not people were paying attention to her, was staring at her daughters as if they were strangers.

"What has gotten into you?" She asked, looking at Heather and Nicole like she might cry.

Turning to her sister she said tearfully, "Addie, I know we have had our rivalry, but please know I had no idea this was happening."

My mom had been silent this entire time. She appeared to be lost in thought.

She spoke up finally, firmly but not angrily. "There is a lot going on here than I can't understand or even want to understand. But I feel I am partly to blame, we all are." She spoke to Nicole and Heather who were now trying to look at Emily's lit up phone, pretending not to pay attention. "You two are behaving foolishly, putting your own spite and jealousy and desire for quick cash ahead of good sense."

They looked up, chastened. "And Emily, you need to have better judgement than to follow these two silly creatures." She added, standing and holding her hand out for Emily's phone also. She reluctantly handed it over.

Our mom continued, looking at her little sister. "But Etta, I should have tried harder. We both should have. We were both so caught up in our fame, in our rivalry, in competing with one another to see who could achieve more, that we forgot to help our daughters get to know each other."

Aunt Etta nodded. "I spent too many holidays with friends in Hollywood, we should have gotten together more often."

Our mom sat back down next to her sister and patted her on the arm. "I'm sorry. I'm so glad you are near us now. We will make this work."

Erica wasn't going to give up quite so easily. Standing in front of our three younger cousins she took a deep breath. "I apologize for not including you more too. I am sorry for not making more of an effort to get you VIP admission to backstage events and clubs with me. But if you had simply spoken to me about it things could have been so much different. We are cousins, we should be friends. If you want to try again, I will always be polite to you. But if you ever try to take my picture again I will break your phone."

And with that uncharacteristically forceful speech, she breezed past them and into the house, leaving all of us staring after her.

After everyone had left, I went upstairs to see how Erica was doing. I found her pacing in her room, agitated though taking deep breaths as though trying to calm herself. She was dressed for a workout in a pair of black shorts that showed off her perfect yoga butt, a colorful tank top, and her wind breaker.

"That was intense." I said to her, as I watched her lace up her shoes.

"I know! I've felt guilty ever since our European tour when Heather wanted to work as our PR manager. I tried to let her down gently, but Tonya has done our advertising and media practically since the beginning. But taking ugly pictures of me? I hope those don't end up splashed all over the grocery store checkout line!" She said, although she really didn't look too concerned, she'd had pictures of her show up in a tabloid two years earlier with a red nose and messy hair. The headlines screamed the group had kicked her out and she was having a breakdown. All completely untrue. I guess she figured some unattractive angles of her dancing with her sister and a few guys at a small-town bachelor party really wasn't going to be that bad.

"Are you OK?" I asked her. She was still taking in slow deep breaths.

"I'm trying to stay centered and unconcerned," she said. "Even though Charlie responded and we're not going to dinner tonight."

I could tell this really hurt. "Was he rude?"

She was matter of fact. "No, in fact once again he proves himself to be a great guy. He was totally honest and upfront. He just said he doesn't feel comfortable getting any closer since it looks like I'm still working through another relationship. He even said we would talk later."

"That's promising." I said, hoping it really was.

She shrugged, "Maybe. Anyway, I'm going on a walk with Geri and Amanda, do you want to come?"

I grabbed my shoes and walked out the door with her. She seemed determined to stay positive. As we walked down the street she invited me, Pearson, and Perry to join her at the recording session with The Raven and I helped distract her by planning what she should wear.

When we arrived at Geri's, Amanda immediately gave her a quick little hug, right there on the sidewalk. "I always knew we'd be sisters some day!" She squealed. "Charlie came over first thing this morning and told me you two were going to dinner tonight!"

Geri added, "Good, now you really can move home. I need you to keep motivating me to walk anyway."

Erica laughed, though I could hear her pain. "I wish it was all that easy!" She said, "But it looks like Charlie and I still don't have good timing."

The Raven

We arrived at The Aerie studio with a lot of fanfare. Our mom had insisted on coming and she entered the well-outfitted studio with a flurry of silky scarves and eager exclamations. A photographer outfitted with an enormous professional camera zeroed in on her as we made our way to the visitor lounge where we would watch the proceedings. Our dad had also come to Los Angeles but was occupied with one of his writing teams so he hadn't joined us. Seeing our mom mug for the camera, I wished he was here too.

I was happy we could bring Pearson and Perry. They were eager to see Carlisle, Ben, The Raven, and all that went into a day at a major recording studio. Angie brought up the rear, her efficiency and business-like bearing was our steadying force. Erica was thrilled to see Carlisle and Ben again. Her two band-mates rushed to her side as soon as she stepped through the door. Jenna and Kelly joined them.

"Are you doing OK?" Ben asked, his blue eyes concerned as he took in her pale face and troubled expression.

Putting her arm around him and leaning briefly into his shoulder she whispered that she was hanging in there.

"What about you?" She asked her friends.

Carlisle shrugged and shook his head, "I was in such a low place for a few days there that Jenna and Ben took me to a health and rejuvenation spa. Jimmy would have hated it...but I have to admit I feel better. I wonder if I'll ever feel really happy again though."

Jenna patted her little brother on the shoulder. "We're thinking we might go back to Walla Walla, maybe spend time with the family."

"Yeah," added Ben, "Los Angeles seems so empty without Jim. It seems like the past few years just flew by, almost like it was someone else's life. I hardly appreciated how good it was before and now it's just," he snapped his fingers, "gone."

The remaining Flying Foes and their friends stood sadly near the entrance for a little longer before Malcolm, who had been across the room talking with a sound technician, came bustling over.

"Here we are, together again!" Malcolm bellowed out. Erica winced at his lack of sensitivity, couldn't he see their sad expressions?

Malcolm bulldozed on, "The Raven is due to be here any moment and she will want to get right to work. I need the three of you to get your instruments ready. Joe's over there, he will take care of you."

He started to walk off, but then turned back to Erica and kissed her quickly on the cheek. "Good to see you, hon," he whispered almost as an afterthought.

She recoiled from him, why had she not noticed what a jerk he was before? She looked at Ben and Carlisle who were both shaking their heads at Malcolm's antics.

"I'm done with him, don't worry," she assured them.

"OK," Ben said suspiciously, "we've heard that before."

"Well you won't hear it again," Erica said holding her head high, "because Malcolm Jamison Smithe is history!"

The Raven was everything we had ever imagined, tall, cool, impeccably-dressed. Her low throaty voice like liquid gold pouring over metal. She was also surprisingly gracious and well-mannered. They began by performed three of her standards. She was then eager to play some of her favorites from The Flying Foes. Erica gave me a thumbs up through the glass, I could tell she was having a great time. We all thought they had created an amazing tribute album. It was when they just let loose and started improvising, though, that things really started to sparkle. The Raven was a true musician and Erica, Carlisle, and Ben fit right in with her style. I could see them relaxing as they enjoyed playing music together. Erica even tossed in a song I'd heard her improvising when she had played with Charlie after we had all gone out. It was magical.

As everybody was wrapping up, we all applauded. I could hear our mom exclaiming to Kelly, Jim's wife, how Jim would have loved this. Kelly nodded, brushing away a tear. I could tell the collaboration had exceeded everyone's expectations. It was great to see Erica, Ben, and Carlisle smiling for a moment. Jim's friends were giving him a wonderful tribute album. As I was helping Erica pack up her guitars and tambourine The Raven asked her about the song she and Charlie had made up.

"I really liked that last one, it was different from the others. More positive." The Raven added. "Did you and Jim write that one together too?"

Erica smiled, looking at me briefly. "No, that was one I made up with a friend from home. He's pretty special to me too."

Just then the door opened and Roxana Shilling Rhodes strode in followed by a manager-type guy in a suit. Roxana! Erica looked up at me through the window where I sat in the observation room. I'm sure we both wore identical expressions of shock and horror. I looked behind her to see if Ricky had dared to show his face too.

So far Ricky had not been charged with Jim's death. Carlisle, Ben, and I were still debating whether we needed to turn him in. He was responsible for Jimmy's death, but so far none of us had been able to bring ourselves to make the call. Turn in my kids' dad? I couldn't do it. Ben and Carlisle didn't want to either, we were all hoping someone else would.

Roxana wore her typical haughty expression, sailing past all of us without even making eye contact. She looked even worse than the last time I had seen her at the night club the night of Jim's death. The circles under her eyes were more pronounced and deep lines ran down from her mouth giving her a perpetual sneer.

"Am I too late? Thanks for giving me this chance Malcolm, hon." I heard her say, stopping by the sound booth to give Malcolm a proprietary peck on the cheek as she sailed by the observation room. The suited guy joined Malcolm, shaking his hand officially.

Malcolm patted Roxana on the butt, looking her thin frame over lasciviously. Scowling out at the rest of the performers, he seemed unconcerned with Erica's sudden discomfort. I was surprised he would have included Roxana in this singing event, she had not performed in any way beyond commercials since her Kids Rock days.

"Don't pack up yet, Miss Schilling is finally here. We're going to do a couple more songs for the tribute." Malcolm called out.

Without so much as a greeting to Erica, Roxana burst onto the stage gave The Raven a peck on each cheek. "Raven!" Roxana drawled, "Looking fabulous. I can't wait to sing our song."

The Raven looked momentarily confused, I wondered if Roxana's arrival was as much of a surprise to her as it was to the rest of us. It looked like Roxana wasn't a complete stranger to The Raven, but they obviously weren't friends either. But The Raven, a true professional, returned a murmured compliment and repositioned her microphone.

Ben and Carlisle looked at Erica who was still standing at her microphone next to The Raven. It was obvious they had not expected to have Roxana barge in on their tribute session and they were both clearly uncomfortable at her presence. Erica looked back at her friends and shrugged slightly, then she looked towards Malcolm raising her eyebrows. I wondered if Malcolm was trying to punish Erica. Was this because she'd been with Charlie?

Malcolm bustled out of the sound booth. "OK, have we all said our hellos?" He asked, not waiting for a response. "Since this is a tribute to Jim, I asked Rox here to join us. She was really eager to share a special song for her old friend."

Roxana smiled demurely, looking up through her dark lashes at Malcolm.

I looked at Kelly, who was sitting next to me. "Jim and Roxana were never friends, right?" I asked her.

She wrinkled her nose, shaking her head. "Not really, he hated how she used to treat Erica. But he put up with her when she married Ricky. I never could stand either one of them, though, so we rarely saw them. And when I finally heard how Ricky treated you...I refused to even hang out with them at all."

"Thanks, that's loyal of you." I said, then I chuckled softly. "I wonder what Roxana had to do to get in on this reunion?"

Kelly rolled her eyes. "I don't. Jim always told me Roxana's favorite way of getting ahead...had something to do with some head."

I smacked her arm. "Kelly!"

She smiled, though it was still tinged with sadness, it was good to see her feisty personality coming out for a moment. "Well...look at Malcolm. Clearly there's something more to this little arrangement than a mere business agreement!"

It was true - Malcolm was now talking to the singers and Roxana was blatantly flirting with him. Erica was trying to keep her face calm, I could tell. But seeing Roxana straighten his tie and wiggle her shoulders while blinking up at him was pretty obnoxious even from our observation room.

But it didn't end there. When Malcolm got Roxana hooked up with a third microphone Roxana pouted.

"But Mal...this was supposed to be just me and The Raven with Jim's guys." She wailed, looking at Erica out of the corner of her eye.

Erica didn't even wait to hear what Malcolm had to say. She held up her hands and went toward the exit.

"Hey, don't worry about me! I'm happy with the songs we've done." Erica said stepping toward the exit. Then she stopped, her hand on the door. She seemed to be debating. She took a deep breath and spoke again, it came out a little rushed. "And Roxana, I have no respect for you. I would never choose to sing with you again."

Roxana's face registered anger for a brief second before she rearranged her expression into pitiful hurt. She looked at Malcolm as if expecting him to speak up for her, but he seemed as surprised as the rest of us to see Erica speaking up for herself.

From our observation room Angie turned to me with a huge grin on her face. "Finally!" She whispered. She then got up and followed Erica out the door into the lobby.

I was pleased to see Ben and Carlisle moving away from their instruments too.

"Hey, man, I got stuff to do." Carlisle said, grabbing his sticks and walking towards us.

"Yeah, I wasn't prepared for this." Ben added, joining us in the observation room.

Roxana kept her face still, as if the Flying Foes refusing to play with her was not a big deal. She shrugged her shoulders at The Raven, shaking her head.

The Raven looked like she was about to walk out too, she pulled her phone out of her pocket and was about to check it. But Malcolm quickly burst to action, shouting orders, getting some piped-in music started. The Raven held her hands up, looking over at her manager who just shrugged. Before The Raven had a chance to do anything Roxana started singing along with the music. It was one of The Flying Foes early songs, one Erica and Jim had written. It sounded ridiculous for Roxana to be singing, her voice was thin and she was off key. The Raven seemed to decide to help her. She joined in, pulling Roxana to the right notes. The Raven's rich voice nearly made the song bearable, but Roxana's nasally voice ruined the overall sound.

The Raven only put up with one song. Pulling her cell phone out again, she gave a quick apology before joining her manager and publicist. Roxana was left alone, her mouth open in indignation. She put her hands on her hips.

"Uh, Malcolm?" She said angrily. "What is going on?"

Malcolm loosened his tie, ran over to her, and whispered. He must have made up for the short recording session, because she smiled and nodded. She then sang one on her own. I'm not a musician, but it was awful. The lyrics were trite and repetitive and her voice hurt my ears.

I wished Erica could have been there, she would have enjoyed seeing Roxana's silly performance. But she didn't come in until after Roxana had finished her song. Despite Roxana's rude treatment, Erica held her head high. I think she was proud of herself for not letting Roxana or Malcolm push her around. Seeing that no one else was on stage, Erica came into the observation room with the rest of us.

"What was that?" She asked me.

I shook my head, "I think Malcolm was just trying to make you mad. A gentleman to the end. I'm just glad Ricky isn't here."

Once Roxana was smiling again, Malcolm started shouting out that the photographers needed everyone to get posed for their final photo shoot. As Erica listened to him hollering to no one and everyone, completely unconcerned about what other people were feeling, she looked at me and rolled her eyes. I was glad to see she had finally gotten the point. Then she held up a finger and excused herself, pulling out her phone.

"What are you doing?" Malcolm demanded as she headed out of the room back toward the lobby.

She looked up at him without expression and said, "Excuse me, I'm getting an important phone call."

I saw her face brighten as she pushed open the door.

"Hi Charlie," I heard her say, her voice softening. "It's good to hear from you again. I'm at the studio in L.A."

Then she moved further into the lobby, Malcolm began yelling at everyone else, and I began helping to organize Ben and Carlisle for the final photo.

When Erica returned a couple seconds later I could tell the conversation had gone well. Her face was flushed and she was wearing a big smile. She slid into the group, prepared for the group photo. The Raven, with her long legs, stood in the middle of the back, flanked by Carlisle and Ben who were just a couple of inches taller than her. Erica fit perfectly between Ben and The Raven. Roxana was on the other side of The Raven, next to Carlisle. It was a nice arrangement.

But once again, Roxana was not satisfied.

"Malcolm." She whined. "I can't see the photographer. I need to be next to The Raven."

Malcolm was busy conferring with Roxana's publicist, not really paying attention. "Sure, sure." He said. "Yes, Erica why don't you grab that chair right there and sit down in the front?"

Erica narrowed her eyes. If she sat below everyone else she wouldn't look like she was really part of the group. I could see her debating whether or not to say anything. The Raven looked at her and shrugged questioningly, shaking her head in confusion. The way they were already standing looked good. The iconic singer was clearly getting as annoyed as the rest of the group. Erica shook her head.

Our mom looked at Angie. "Do something!" She hissed. "Maybe you could go get that Roxana out of there."

Angie was about to stand up when The Raven spoke up.

"Excuse me," she said politely, her commanding voice capturing everyone's attention. "But I'd prefer to just get a shot with The Flying Foes to start." She smiled kindly at Roxana, "We'll do one at the end with you."

Roxana couldn't argue with The Raven. Pouting, she stomped off the stage, leaving the true performers to have their picture taken.

I saw The Raven smile at Erica who returned a grateful smile in return. In comfortable seats a few feet away, my family and I relaxed. Angie was always very effective at getting things taken care of for Erica, but she also made a pretty good scene.

Percy and Pearson were enjoying all of it, being young boys they had barely registered the arrival of Roxana. Joe had invited Perry into the sound room to listen to the playbacks and he was enjoying the advanced equipment. Pearson had gone onto the stage and had picked up one of the guitars, he was playing softly, enjoying the quality instrument.

The Flying Foes were so occupied with smiling for the cameras with The Raven that they barely noticed the door open and Ricky slip in. He looked worse than I had ever seen him. He was thin and unkempt with an uncharacteristic beard and grubby black tee-shirt and dirty jeans. Perry saw him right away, his young face breaking into a big grin.

"Dad!" He said, practically running out of the sound stage.

My mom and I looked at each other and sighed in unison. We were used to my boys being thrilled with their dad, no matter what his condition. Although I was not happy with him and avoided him completely, I was glad my sons thought he was a good person. At least they lived in the delusion that they had a good dad.

I had to give it to Ricky, at least he pretended for them. Giving Perry an exaggerated hug, he exclaimed loudly how much he had missed him. Then he searched around until he found me. I was still sitting in my comfortable chair next to Kelly in the observation room. I lifted my hand in a half-hearted greeting, I was so furious about the night at The Fountain and Jim that I could barely look at him. Ricky hated having people be mad at him, which was ridiculous considering how many people he had made angry.

Flashing a sad smile, Ricky nodded slowly at me before walking toward where Roxana was talking to Malcolm and her publicist. Roxana, leaning flirtatiously against Malcolm, quickly removed her hand from his chest when she saw Ricky.

She murmured something to Ricky, giving him a loose-armed hug.

Ricky gave her a quick hug, then continued on toward where Pearson was playing the guitar. Erica, Ben, and Carlisle were still smiling and laughing for the photographer, but when Carlisle looked up and saw Pearson his face abruptly changed. He shook his head.

"No, not happening." He said, glaring at Ricky. Narrowing his piercing blue eyes, Carlisle nodded an apology at the photographer before stepping toward Ricky.

Ricky, who was now talking to both Pearson and Perry about the different instruments, didn't notice Carlisle coming toward him.

"How dare you show your face here." Carlisle said, his anger making his voice carry throughout the studio.

Ricky looked up guiltily. "Carlisle - I, I'm so sorry. I wanted to stop. So did he."

Ben too, moved away from the photo session and towards Carlisle and Ricky. Smiling apologetically at Pearson and Perry, he stood next to Carlisle. "Ricky, what you did was unforgivable." Ben said, his normally cheerful face pushed into a scowl.

I stood up and ran out to join them, followed closely by my mom, Angie, and Erica.

Ricky looked briefly at his sons before looking at the ground guiltily. "I know." He said. "That's why I'm here. I called the police just before I came. I turned myself in. I just couldn't live with myself any longer. Jim didn't deserve to die and it was an accident. We were only having fun."

Roxana, who was now standing next to him, chimed in. "Yeah, we loved Jim too. We never meant to hurt him. We couldn't have known the smack was so strong. It had been too long for him and it was too much."

Ricky looked at me. "I have done so much I regret. Pen, I'm so sorry. Please, please forgive me."

I was shocked. In all our years apart, he had never once apologized or even acknowledged the pain he had caused. Though I was used to his false kindness with our boys and I had long ago given up trusting him, his green eyes were sincere. Though he had done so much I couldn't just let him off the hook, like he had done nothing. He had destroyed our lives, he had killed Jim.

Yet - his apology was sincere, I had been married to him and I saw the boy I had loved. Looking into his eyes, I softened. "Thank-you, Ricky." I said, feeling my heart wrench. Then I turned away so no one would see my tears.

As I moved away, my mom and Angie put their arms around me, giving me comfort as they directed me back to the observation room. I heard Ricky giving Kelly an apology, though she wasn't nearly as accepting as me.

"Oh, Ricky," She sighed, "You can apologize all you want. It will never bring my Jim back. I hope you go to jail."

Kelly spun on her heel, grabbed her purse while giving us a quick smile, and slammed the door as she left the studio.

Ricky stood, next to Roxana, as Ben and Carlisle also moved away from him. I could tell he wasn't getting the acceptance he desired, though both Perry and Pearson stayed near him. He was obviously distraught, though I didn't know how he could make up for the injury he had caused. Giving his sons hugs, he wiped a tear from his eyes before saying goodbye and following Roxana from the studio.

As he left he looked into the conference room where I stood with Ben, Carlisle, Angie, and my mom. He spoke one more time. "I am truly sorry, for everything I did to you. I have no excuse, you deserve so much better. All of you."

Then he turned and strode out.

Return

Erica only wanted to stop at her house long enough to pack a fresh suitcase. She had been so comfortable in Walla Walla that she decided to return with us. Our mom was thrilled, and immediately began planning a remodel to Erica's bedroom suite.

"What are we going to do?" Ben had asked, looking at his bandmates of twenty years. "I know with Jim…gone…we can't hope to perform anymore. But what now?"

We had stayed behind in the studio after everyone left. Our mom, Angie, Pearson, and Perry were meeting us at Erica's house and Erica and the guys were packing up their instruments. Jenna, and I were helping as well as we could.

Carlisle didn't even hesitate. "We're going with you, Erica. I miss home. I don't know if I can ever live there again, but I'm ready for a change of pace for awhile."

Ben nodded, "Yeah, that place would be pretty chill for a few days. Sure. I'll go too."

So it was decided. The Flying Foes were no longer a complete band, but they could stay together as much as possible. By the time we all arrived in Walla Walla the next day Erica had already started talking about playing a small concert. Before any of us knew what was happening she was texting their manager,

Joe, and getting things arranged. I knew they would never be the same, but I could tell they were all slowly healing.

I pulled up at our house and was surprised to see Charlie's truck in front. Erica and I both looked at each other and I could tell by her big smile that she was happy to see him.

"Hey Aunt Erica," Pearson said teasingly, pointing at the porch from the back seat. "Isn't that your friend?"

Erica laughed as she got out of the car. "Thanks Pearson. Yes, my friend must have something he wants to say to me."

My dad looked over at Charlie and nodded slightly. Though he didn't have much to say, I could tell he approved. Our mom was busily passing luggage from the truck to Pearson and Perry to carry inside and didn't pay much attention to the sweet scene going on just a few feet away on the front porch.

Erica had approached Charlie slowly, as if unsure what to say. He had been knocking on the front door when we first stopped and when he saw her he stepped down the stairs, meeting her in a big hug.

"I'm sorry." I heard him say. "I have waited for you too long, I don't want to wait any longer."

I didn't hear Erica's reply, but I could tell by the big hug she gave him that she was glad to be with him.

Hometown Gig

"Are you ready?" Erica whispered to Carlisle and Ben as we pulled up to Main Street Studio, the upscale club in downtown Walla Walla. Both grinned before jumping out of our mom's Gran Marquis. They were playing their first concert since Jimmy's death and they were feeling good about it. Our whole family was going to be there, even our cousins. When we had gotten home Erica had been surprised to receive a letter from Heather. A real, actual written-on-stationery apology letter. And Nicole had called Erica and apologized. And Emily had sent her a text, inviting her to lunch. She had even apologized in person. Erica told me she didn't entirely trust them yet, but she was grateful they were trying and she was going to try too. I had vowed to be friendly too - though I was going to be on the lookout.

I was so happy for these guys, they sounded great! Erica looked beautiful dancing up on stage, her face was lit up in a smile as she looked over at Charlie singing along with her. I could tell the crowd loved it. In the three weeks we had been home Erica had been spending a lot of time with Charlie. He had been playing the guitar and singing with her, Carlisle and Ben. The two songs he had played with the group had been excellent and I could tell the crowd enjoyed him.

Even Kelly was there, she was standing at a tall table near the front with Jenna, Geri, Amanda and me. Kelly had decided to move from Los Angeles back to Portland where she could live near her family and had only had to drive a few hours to come up for the show.

For the next song Erica spoke somberly into the microphone. "This one is dedicated to our dear friend Jimmy. We love you Jim, we send this one up to you."

The ballad was beautiful, so unlike what The Flying Foes had been known for, but somehow reminiscent of the fun and freedom they always represented. I could tell the audience was moved, everyone just froze and stared at Erica and the guys. I closed my eyes and just felt the beauty of the music move through me.

I felt a small touch on my forearm. Turning, I was surprised to see Raymond, standing next to me. I looked for his wife, but I didn't see her. It was too loud to talk, but I was so happy he was there. I couldn't help myself from giving him a little hug, leaning into his strong body. He pointed to the next table, where he had been sitting with some friends from school. We waved, smiling.

Raymond looked down at me, giving me a warm friendly smile that brought back memories of all the conversations we had shared years before. Conversations that never went anywhere. Then he looked back up at the stage, clearly enjoying the music. When Erica finished she told the crowd to take a breather, they'd be back. Then she hopped off stage and came running toward us.

"So? What did you think? Too sad?" She asked me, barely registering Raymond.

"You sound absolutely wonderful." I told her, giving her a hug.

Carlisle joined us too. I was surprised. Normally Carlisle slipped outside during breaks and avoided everyone. But I quickly realized why: Amanda. He stood behind her and asked if she had paid the bartender for the extra candle fee.

Looking at the flickering votive, Amanda quickly reached for her purse to pay the ridiculous fee. "Oh! I hadn't realized." She said, flustered.

Everyone laughed. Amanda looked up and saw Carlisle and her face broke into a wide smile.

"Carlisle! You always could get me!" She gave him a big hug and soon they disappeared outside.

Raymond smiled at Erica. "Great job. I saw your flyer and came out to see you. I'm glad I did."

She cocked her head and looked at him closely. "Are you Raymond Nelson?" She asked. I could feel her stepping on my toe. I kicked her a little.

He nodded.

She reached out and took his hand, shaking it vigorously. "It is a pleasure to finally meet you. My sister always valued your friendship." Now I stepped on her foot. She was clearly full of energy and adrenaline from the start of a really good show. I met Raymond's eye and shook my head, smiling. He smiled back.

"OK, well I need some water. I'll talk to you later." She bustled off, leaving us alone.

"Valued my friendship, huh?" Raymond asked.

I laughed. Our friendship had never consisted of anything more than the occasional class project in high school, one evening of long conversation and hand-holding, and a few months of running into each other around town.

I shook my head. "Sorry, she's probably confused."

He took my hand and looked at me intensely. "Can we talk?"

I gulped, though years had passed, I still felt nervous around him. Not to mention - "Aren't you married?"

He shook his head. "No, we just weren't connecting anymore. We signed and made everything official over a year ago. It's been amicable, we share custody of the kids."

Still holding his hand, I followed him outside.

He smiled and looked down at me. I could feel my heart beat faster.

"I kind of hoped you'd call me, or maybe even…write me a note?" He suddenly looked bashful. He kicked at a rock on the ground then met my gaze again.

"A note?" I asked incredulously. "Why would I write you a note?"

"Oh Penny, I always wanted to talk to you. You put that note in my binder all those years ago, about how you thought I was a hero. But I never could talk to you. I couldn't hardly talk to anyone."

I was still just stuck there, with my mouth open. "You got that note?" I felt myself relaxing, not worrying so much about what he was going to think about what I said. He had always been as nervous as me. I put my hand on his big solid chest and smiled up at him.

"You were supposed to write me back! Something about how you had always liked me."

He put his hand over mine, then grabbed my other hand. "Is it too late? I came here tonight hoping you would be here."

"No," I said, stepping toward him, "It's not too late."

He leaned down and whispered, "Penny, I have always liked you."

And before I could respond he tilted my head back and kissed me.

When we went back in Erica and the guys were playing a fast song and people were dancing. Raymond grabbed my hand

and pulled me out onto the dance floor, laughing I joined him. Pretty soon everyone was dancing, even my parents. I looked up at Raymond and smiled, then I looked over at my sister and she winked at me. I was so happy she was home.

Sara Van Donge lives in Walla Walla with her large, fun family. Besides writing she enjoys biking, yoga, and cooking. When she has time, Sara collects advanced degrees and teaches Spanish, reading, and writing.

Her passion for her hometown is evident in her previous books, 'I Love Love Walla Walla' and 'Dutch Jo's Good Time Girls' available now on Amazon. For more information on her latest projects and to sign up for her mailing list, go to her website at platformpublishers.com.